HAUNTED
CHATHAM

HAUNTED
CHATHAM

Neil Arnold

The
History
Press

I would like to dedicate this book
to my sister Vicki − I love you x

The stories grew more and more lurid, wilder and sillier, and soon
the gasps and cries merged into fits of choking laughter …

Susan Hill − *The Woman in Black*

First published 2012

The History Press
The Mill, Brimscombe Port
Stroud, Gloucestershire, GL5 2QG
www.thehistorypress.co.uk

© Neil Arnold, 2012

The right of Neil Arnold to be identified as the Author
of this work has been asserted in accordance with the
Copyrights, Designs and Patents Act 1988.

British Library Cataloguing in Publication Data.
A catalogue record for this book is available from the British Library.

ISBN 978 0 7524 6173 1
Typesetting and origination by The History Press
Printed in Great Britain

Contents

I did not believe in ghosts. Or rather, until this day, I had not done so, and whatever stories I had heard of them I had, like most rational, sensible young men, dismissed as nothing more than stories indeed.

Susan Hill – *The Woman in Black*

Acknowledgements

Many thanks to the following for helping me write this book: My mum Paulene, and dad, Ron; my sister Vicki; my wife Jemma; my nan, Win, and granddad, Ron; Joe Chester; Sean Tudor; Missy Lindley and Corriene Vickers; The History Press; Chatham World Heritage; the *Kent Messenger*; Adscene; the *Chatham, Rochester & Gillingham News*; *Kent Today*; the *Chatham Observer*; the *Medway Messenger*; *This Is Kent*; *True Crime*; the *Evening Post*; the *Chatham Standard*. Big thanks also to Medway Archives & Local Studies; *Paranormal Magazine*; *Most Haunted*; Chris Cooke; Derek Hargrave; Matt Newton; Susie Higgins and Mark Gower; Mark Wright; Maureen; Judy at City Books, Rochester; Lisa Birch; Rachel Thomson-King; Shane Nichols at Fort Amherst; and Terry Cameron. Extra special thanks to Pam Wood at Chatham Dockyard and the people of Chatham who came forward with their ghostly tales. Thanks to Simon Wyatt for the illustrations. All photographs are by the author unless otherwise stated.

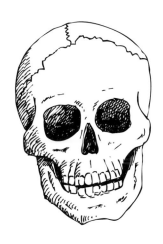

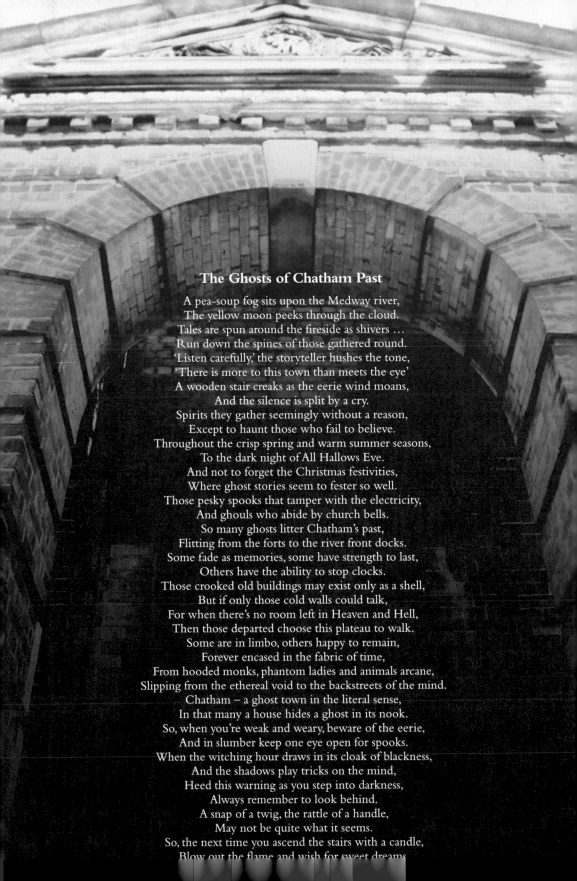

The Ghosts of Chatham Past

A pea-soup fog sits upon the Medway river,
The yellow moon peeks through the cloud.
Tales are spun around the fireside as shivers …
Run down the spines of those gathered round.
'Listen carefully,' the storyteller hushes the tone,
'There is more to this town than meets the eye'
A wooden stair creaks as the eerie wind moans,
And the silence is split by a cry.
Spirits they gather seemingly without a reason,
Except to haunt those who fail to believe.
Throughout the crisp spring and warm summer seasons,
To the dark night of All Hallows Eve.
And not to forget the Christmas festivities,
Where ghost stories seem to fester so well.
Those pesky spooks that tamper with the electricity,
And ghouls who abide by church bells.
So many ghosts litter Chatham's past,
Flitting from the forts to the river front docks.
Some fade as memories, some have strength to last,
Others have the ability to stop clocks.
Those crooked old buildings may exist only as a shell,
But if only those cold walls could talk,
For when there's no room left in Heaven and Hell,
Then those departed choose this plateau to walk.
Some are in limbo, others happy to remain,
Forever encased in the fabric of time,
From hooded monks, phantom ladies and animals arcane,
Slipping from the ethereal void to the backstreets of the mind.
Chatham – a ghost town in the literal sense,
In that many a house hides a ghost in its nook.
So, when you're weak and weary, beware of the eerie,
And in slumber keep one eye open for spooks.
When the witching hour draws in its cloak of blackness,
And the shadows play tricks on the mind,
Heed this warning as you step into darkness,
Always remember to look behind.
A snap of a twig, the rattle of a handle,
May not be quite what it seems.
So, the next time you ascend the stairs with a candle,
Blow out the flame and wish for sweet dreams.

Foreword

You must know at least one ghost story, stepfather, everyone knows one ...

Susan Hill – *The Woman in Black*

It was in the late 1960s, when my family and I moved to an old large, army building to live, that I saw a ghost. I was just eleven years old at the time. Based on my description, it was decided that what I had seen could have been a nurse from about the time of the Crimean War. It added to the obsession that I had then, which still remains with me to this day. The curious need to research ghost stories and track down any real facts still holds its fascination. I knew of a drummer boy ghost yarn as a child and now, as an adult, I have researched the real murder. Putting meat on the bones of a story, if you pardon the expression, gives me a great deal of satisfaction. The real journey is making the past come to life and giving it a voice; the ghost walks do just that for me, whilst giving those long dead a chance to 'air their views' once more.

There are ghosts in the Dockyard – but why do we have so many? This has caused much debate; the earliest reference to a ghost in the yard was from Samuel Pepys. It is easy to imagine that on dimly lit, misty, eerie evenings, ghost stories and tales of mysterious noises and footsteps are recounted to help wile away a night shift. Today we are left with an 80-acre site; the majority of the buildings were constructed between 1704 and 1855, and were used for shipbuilding during the magnificent age of sail. It is no wonder that the legacy of the military and the colourful past of the shipwrights has left their footprints behind, echoing down the cobblestone roads of the present.

Some stories have been handed down, and the ghosts not only want their stories to be retold, they also let us know that they are there. Using all their senses on a ghost investigation, people have detected sudden drops in room temperature and odours, such as the smell of horses, fresh hay, and urine – but also more pleasant aromas like roses, lavender and even freshly ironed linen. Footsteps have been heard when no one was there. Tour groups have even heard heavy objects being dropped, when they were the only people in the building at the time. Raw emotions, like a sense of overwhelming sadness, have been experienced by visitors; I have seen grown men cry in Commissioner's House and people run from the building weeping. However, sometimes these feelings are on the other end of the spectrum; I have been told many times that the atmosphere evokes a feeling of anger in some people during the course of a tour. The attic space is well-known for having a spooky atmosphere and the joiner's shop was where, twenty-two years ago, I first heard a ghost in the yard. Recently, when I gave a talk to the present tenants, they confirmed that these incidents were continuing to happen.

I grew up in Chatham and remember the area which was known as the Brook; I am even lucky enough to own pictures of the people who lived and worked in old Chatham. My grandmother would tell me of the town of her youth and the stories in our family date back to the 1850s.

Every year new stories and ghostly goings-on come to light. Neil has looked at all aspects of the Dockyard stories and of Chatham, unearthing an excellent selection of ghost stories. I hope you enjoy reading them as much as I have.

Pam Wood, 2012

Pam Wood is Visitor Services Manager at Chatham Dockyard and organises regular ghost tours around the site. For more information visit www.theDockyard.co.uk

Introduction

In AD 880, the town that we now know as Chatham appeared as Cetham – the name deriving from the British root ceto and the Old English 'ham', meaning a forest settlement. However, author Edwin Harris states that the name Chatham supposedly derives from the Saxon word *cyte* – meaning a cottage, and again 'ham'. The Domesday Book of 1086 records the town as Ceteham, while Harris also records that it was known as Cettham. Many centuries later, Chatham harbours no forest whatsoever.

Chatham is most famous for its Historic Dockyard, situated on the River Medway, which was established as a Royal Dockyard in 1568 to help support the navy. The Dockyard was closed in 1984 as a naval resource, but it still exists to support local businesses and hosts events; it also attracts thousands of tourists each year.

The town also harbours the famously haunted Fort Amherst, as well as several other forts. It boasts a busy high street, a railway station, and its own football team. Today, more than 50,000 people reside in Chatham. One of the town's most famous residents was author Charles Dickens, who lived there as a boy, first at Ordnance Terrace from 1817 to 1821, and then in the Brook from 1821 to 1823.

I was born in the town in October 1974 to my amazing parents, and spent more than thirty years there. I grew up on a housing estate, and whilst much of my childhood was spent playing football, watching horror films or getting up to no good, I've also always written stories. I've always been intrigued by local mysteries – I was heavily influenced by the fishing trips my dad and I took to the local, murky lakes in pursuit of mythical monster fish – and whilst Chatham may not have the rural atmosphere of say, Ashford, or the cobbled quirks of neighbouring Rochester, it is still steeped in history. The town has clearly moved on from the time when it was a small village that sat on the banks of the river. For me, history has always walked hand in hand with ghost stories, so it's no surprise that many phantoms are said to haunt the town when one considers the amount of human remains that have been disturbed from their ancient resting places over the years. For instance, in March 1897, during the construction of a new store at Slicketts Hill, eleven ancient graves were exposed. Meanwhile, on 8 November 1950, the *Chatham Standard* reported that Anglo-Saxon remains had been discovered at Kitchener Barracks. The find, dating back to the 'fourth or fifth century', consisted of six skeletons which had also been dug up two centuries before. Five years later, the remains of Napoleonic soldiers were found by workmen digging behind a shop in Chatham High Street. These macabre finds instilled within me a need for atmospheric tales.

Most of the stories that you are about to read are previously unpublished. Indeed, many are first-hand accounts of the witnesses. Others have come from old newspaper clippings and different archived sources. Some are in-depth reports, others vague. Over the years I've collected literally hundreds of ghost stories pertaining to Chatham, but space does not allow me to feature every one, so I hope you enjoy those that I have chosen. Some relate to my own family and friends – people I trust. Other stories shed new light on those classic Chatham cases, i.e. Fort Amherst, the Theatre Royal and Chatham's historic Dockyard – for the first time ever the legends of these three locations can now be looked at in-depth. The book also touches on a few cases that could be deemed as downright weird.

At the time of writing I live in neighbouring Rochester, but it has been a delight revisiting my childhood haunts. Seeing some of those once ghost-infested places brought to mind The Beatles' song, 'In My Life'. Traipsing through the streets of Chatham brought back childhood memories as once again – with camera in hand – I slipped through holes in snagging fences, climbed over crumbling walls, slinked between pallid gravestones, and entered locations I knew I was not permitted to be in. The rush of excitement was added to by the fact that these were the places I once knew to be haunted. Of course, some of these once eerie locations only exist as memory – they've since given way to modern construction – but other places have maintained their atmospheric charm. For those of you visiting such places, I do not advise following the child within you and trespassing, instead please ask permission from landowners etc., before embarking on any ghost hunts!

I do not expect you to believe all the tales contained within this book, because, let's face it, ghosts have always been an unproven mystery – they seemingly exist, if they exist at all, as half-hinted forms and yet so many people claim to have observed them. It is important to enjoy such yarns, made all the more atmospheric when told around a flickering log fire on a crisp autumnal night. For those who do believe in such stories, *Haunted Chatham* will provide a glimpse into one of Kent's most historic locations; and for those of you who remain unconvinced of such spook tales, I can only hope that as you doze off to sleep after this adventure, that some hideous spectre doesn't infiltrate your nightmares and force you to question your disbelief. And remember, a ghost story is for life … not just for Christmas. So, as presenter Nick Ross used to say on BBC's *Crimewatch*, 'don't have nightmares!'

Neil Arnold, 2012

About the Author

Neil Arnold is a full-time monster hunter and the author of several books, including *Haunted Rochester, Haunted Ashford, Haunted Maidstone, Paranormal Kent, Paranormal London, Mystery Animals of the British Isles: Kent* and *Shadows in the Sky: The Haunted Airways of Britain*.

He has worked with the BBC, ITV, Channel 4, Sky and NBC, appeared on radio across the world, and written articles for magazines such as *Fortean Times, Paranormal, Ghost Voices* and *Fate*.

Neil runs monthly ghost walks at Blue Bell Hill (www.bluebellhillghostwalk.blogspot.com) and Rochester (www.hauntedrochester.blogspot.com). He is also a lecturer on folklore and mystery animals, and for many years has run Kent Big Cat Research, investigating sightings of 'big cats' in the south-eastern countryside.

The author.

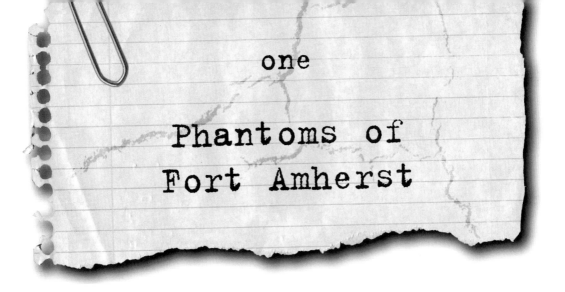

one

Phantoms of Fort Amherst

I had always thought that ghostly apparitions and similar strange occurrences always seemed to be experienced at several removes, by someone who had known someone who had heard it from someone they knew!

Susan Hill – *The Woman in Black*

Fort Amherst – situated on Dock Road and within a few hundred yards of Chatham's Dockyard – is Britain's largest Napoleonic fortress. When the Dutch ran riot along the River Medway in 1667, Chatham Dockyard was raided due to a lack of defence. Work began on a fort in 1755: some forty-seven years after the original plans were laid out. The site on which the fortress was constructed harboured several caves and over time these were lengthened and strengthened to form the impressive labyrinth of tunnels one can see today. According to the Fort Amherst website:

> To ensure the protection of the Dockyard, three defendable gateways were constructed to control and defend access into the area protected by the Chatham

Lines. One of these gateways, the Upper Barrier Guardhouse, can be found within the lower portion of Fort Amherst. The guardhouse housed a small garrison to defend the route from Chatham town by the use of a drawbridge, loop-holed walls and a set of three heavy gates. The barrack rooms within this building have been restored for your enjoyment.

The fort, despite existing as a formidable defence system, was never put into use during battle. The website adds that: 'In 1820 the defences were declared obsolete due to better artillery equipment with a greater firing range.' Even so, during the Victorian period thousands flocked to the fort to watch training exercises, and during the Second World War the winding tunnels were used by the Anti-Invasion Planning Unit and Civil Defence. It wasn't until the 1970s that the fort was restored. Volunteers, with the permission of the Ministry of Defence, clearly felt that the fort had a lot to offer as a tourist attraction, and in 1980 Fort Amherst was purchased from the MOD by the Fort Amherst & Lines Trust. Parts of the fort are now open to the public and the regular ghost tours are among the most popular attractions.

On 30 October 1990 the *Chatham Standard* reported, 'Ghostie tour a sell-out', stating:

Spine-chilling scenes with hideous apparitions and ghouls confronted people brave enough to book places on the Halloween tours of Fort Amherst, which got off to an early start this weekend. Around 2,700 people will have been daring enough to set foot in the creepy caves below the Napoleonic fort after the last tour tomorrow (Wednesday) night … The fort custodian, Mr John Loudwell, said the interest in the Halloween tunnel tours was increasing year by year and this year's were a sell out before the weekend.

Volunteers guide the reckless visitors around the fort's subterranean chambers for the half-hour tour – if their nerves can stand it long enough. And even the bravest no doubt cast a wary eye over one shoulder for the little drummer boy who is said to haunt the fort.

Fort Amherst, along with Pluckley in Ashford (see my *Haunted Ashford* book), is recognised as one of the most haunted places in Kent. Each year thousands of people flock to the area. In 2008 staff of local radio station KMFM decided to test their nerves with a vigil at the fort; their story was covered by the *Medway Messenger* on 7 November under the headline: 'Spooky night in tunnels tests our fear of ghosts.'

Fort Amherst has a haunted reputation.

Amherst tunnels, visible from the main road.

Thousands of people were left spooked after tuning in to KMFM for Medway's Halloween broadcast on Friday night. But spare a thought for presenters Oli Kemp, Vanessa Elms and Rob Wills – the chosen trio – who spent the night looking for other restless souls deep within the haunted tunnels of Fort Amherst …

Presenter Oli Kemp recorded his nightly investigation for the newspaper, writing:

When I first mentioned to my colleagues Vanessa and Rob that we should do a live ghost hunt for Halloween, you should have seen the look of terror on their faces. But when I promised them they wouldn't be alone they slowly came around to the idea. Alongside two mediums, a historian and a group of ghost experts, the three of us made our way to haunted Fort Amherst in Chatham. Were we sceptical about the event we lovingly called Frightday Night? I think it's fair to say we all were, but the thought of seeing paranormal activity certainly got the adrenaline pumping. The dark spooky tunnels, built to defend the Royal Dockyard from attack by Napoleon's forces, were enough to send chills down your spine on their own, so imagine what it was like when medium Richard Ware made contact with a dark and evil spirit called Vincent in the Guard House.

Nice, quiet Richard was suddenly shouting and egging Vincent on, which was slightly unnerving. While I wanted Vincent to 'show his face', as it were, at the same time I was kind of hoping he wouldn't. He didn't sound like a man to be messed with. Vincent did eventually reveal his presence by dropping something on the floor and making everyone jump. Richard also mentioned the presence of a woman called Margaret and a man called Frank. The names didn't mean anything to Vanessa and I, but it suddenly dawned on Rob that they were the names of his dead aunt and uncle. Was it a coincidence, or were Rob's dead relatives really trying to get through to him? I guess we'll never know.

The newspaper article concluded with the mention of motion sensors and other gadgets that were being employed to monitor the atmosphere. Although different temperatures were recorded, and EVP (Electronic Voice Phenomena) equipment was used, it seems that like many a ghost hunt, it was minds, rather than ghosts, that were running wild.

In many ghost hunts, especially those involving a medium, it seems as though whilst some alleged spirits are contacted, or known to make their presence felt, these are often completely unconnected with the actual location. These reputed ghosts could well be connected to any member of the audience, or indeed the medium in question, and whilst strange noises, fleeting shadows and fluctuating temperatures seem unusual, they are clearly not concrete evidence of paranormal activity.

A number of ghostly investigations have been conducted at Fort Amherst. The Ghost Connections team visited the fort a few years ago; this resulted in, according to their website, one investigator, named Dave, seeing a dark figure. The sound of footfalls and the feeling of something

Entrance tunnel into the belly of the fort.

pressing were also recorded, as well as whispering voices, the sight of a dark mass and a sudden drop in temperature. In today's climate, this type of activity seems relatively common, and with such places harbouring so much energy, one would almost expect such occurrences. On another occasion the fort was visited by Ghost Search UK, who reported sightings of what are known as orbs. These are dubious round forms of possible energy that are often picked up on digital cameras, but they are rarely seen by the naked eye. Sceptics argue that such forms have only existed since the dawn of the digital camera, suggesting that the recording equipment is sensitive to particles of dust, moisture and the like. Many ghost hunters and spiritualists believe that orbs are in fact early spirit form, but this is never likely to be proven.

Fort Amherst, like Chatham Dockyard and the rural village of Pluckley, harbours so many ghost stories that people keep coming back to find them. Although the ghost tours are provided for pure entertainment – I paid a visit there in my teenage years and enjoyed the zombies (which leapt out from crevices) and atmosphere – people do claim to experience strange things at the fort.

I'd always heard, as a child, that the stuffy tunnels of the fort were home to the spirits of Napoleonic soldiers. In fact, the remains of such prisoners of war were unearthed from St Mary's Island, once nicknamed Deadman's Island, just a short way down Dock Road. The find was reported in the 20 November 1990 edition of the *Chatham Standard* under the heading: 'Gruesome finds at toxic site.' The newspaper reported that whilst digging for the present housing estate on the island, hundreds of French soldiers were unearthed and that tight security regulations were imposed to seal off the area. The remains were found at a 300sq.ft site and a mobile mortuary was installed to temporarily house the bodies. The remains, according to a pathologist and the coroner's office, were said to be more than 100 years old and had the potential to support deadly diseases which lived on in the soil. Originally, more than 2,000 bodies were interred at the island in 1869. These had been prisoners who perished due to the appalling conditions on the hulks of the Medway.

Reports dating back several decades alleged that moaning ghosts of war could be heard in the fort, and some visitors reported the sounds of footsteps echoing through the cold passageways. Maybe the ghosts are those of Jutish settlers, whose remains were unearthed during a dig for the foundations of an extension to the fort back in 1779. Legend has it that around thirty years ago a man fainted at the fort after seeing a figure walk through one of the walls. Another rumour doing the rounds many years ago claimed that an electrician, doing some rewiring at the fort, had been pushed over by an invisible presence. Fort Amherst is littered with legends – claims have been made by a naive public that many years ago the pitch-black, damp tunnels were used for Devil worship. Then there are the tales of whispering voices, usually in the ear of unsuspecting victims; the photographs of 'orbs'; the numerous ghost hunts resulting, allegedly, in various mediums contacting all manner of souls; and those mysterious, if non-specific, voices recorded on tape. Fort Amherst is the sort of place one would expect to see a ghost, or at least feel some type of presence. So, in the autumn of 2011, I decided to contact the fort for a personal guided tour to find out more about the ghostly tales.

On a bright September morning I met up with Shane Nichols, one of the volunteers at the fort, and he kindly agreed to show

Shane Nichols – volunteer at Fort Amherst.

me around. Once inside the gloomy tunnels I was impressed by the almost film set-like design of the imposing walls, and as temperatures fluctuated from room to room – some were as stuffy as hell, others chilled the bone – Shane recounted several eerie tales. We began at a tunnel which led us to what is known as the Plotting Room. One could imagine how busy this room would have been in the past, as employees received phone calls from the connecting Communications Room, in order to plot where the enemy bombs were going to drop. According to Shane there are a few ghost stories attached to the Plotting Room. In the past, paranormal investigators recorded sudden extreme drops in temperature, and on one occasion a group of researchers were spooked by a mist which appeared to come from the door leading to the Communications Room.

A figure appeared, dressed in Victorian attire – a long, dark coat and a black top hat – and walked straight through the team of investigators and out through the closed door of the room into the tunnels. The most alarming feature about this spectre was that it was bereft of a face!

As I've already briefly mentioned, there is also a legend concerning an electrician who was allegedly pushed by a spirit some time back; Shane elaborated on the story:

> The electrician was working on a ladder when a fire bucket fell off the wall. The electrician thought nothing of it until the bucket moved of its own accord. The man immediately thought that someone was playing a trick and so took a peek into the tunnels but could find no one present. With that, the bucket flew across the room!

Another bout of paranormal activity took place during a tour of the fort. As a guide was leading a group of visitors out of the Communications Room and into the Plotting Room, he noticed that someone was missing. He went back into the Communications Room – where there are several desks and old phones – and noticed one of the tourists chatting on one of the phones. When the woman had finished talking she said that the phone had rung, and that when she had picked it up a female voice on the other end was telling her that a bomb had dropped on her house. The tour guide knew that this room had been the hub, many years ago, for dealing with such calls from worried residents, but the bizarre thing about the call, as the guide pointed out to the visitor, was the fact that the old phone wasn't connected. It seems that the woman had taken a phantom phone call.

After we came out of the sweat box that was the Communications Room, Shane and I slipped into the chilly area of the well. In this gloomy passageway Shane told me that on several tours, young women have reported having their skirts tugged by an unseen presence. On one occasion, during one of the first ever Fort Amherst ghost tours, a teenage visitor had to leave the tunnel after claiming that some unseen assailant was pestering her. Some believe the ghost is that of a young boy, and a mischievous one at that, who, on occasion, likes to pull the hair of women and slap their buttocks. In the same area there is also vague mention of the sound of drumming and the sporadic sightings of a young boy.

The haunted Plotting Room.

The Communications Room.

The 'angel stone' in Fort Amherst.

Further into the belly of the fort, Shane spoke of the legend of the 'angel stone'. Many years ago it was believed that Napoleonic soldiers dug out the tunnels we see today, but Shane believes this to be untrue and that Cornish and Welsh miners may well have given a helping hand in extending the maze of winding tunnels. The 'angel stone', a stone which juts out of the white wall on the right as you walk through the tunnels, was often touched by miners as a talisman of good luck. The stone has an obscure carving on it, which some believe resembles an angel. Elsewhere in the area there are other scratches of graffiti alongside slightly more morbid inscriptions, which suggest that some of the initials signify people who died and were possibly buried in the tunnels. During the eighteenth century there was said to have been a huge cave-in and many people perished in those cold tunnels, so it's no real surprise that people often claim to see eerie mists. In one area, known as the Lightning Shaft, a female phantom is said to loiter. To the tour operators the ghost is known as 'Lily of the Valley', and she is said to emerge from the white door on the right of the passage. Bizarrely, the woman, dressed in Georgian attire, is said to appear as a beautiful woman to male visitors, whilst any females on the tour who see the lady describe her as ugly!

Before the fort was restored, many years ago, local vandals would break in to cause damage to the tunnels, by lighting fires and scribbling graffiti. Legend has it that one dark night a group of local youths broke into the fort, and once inside they split up in order to carry out their acts of vandalism. Most of the teenagers became spooked by the whispering voices echoing through the passageways, whilst others heard footsteps and so decided to leave the fort. But, according to Shane, the leader of the group wasn't so easily dissuaded

A few decades ago a group of teenagers broke into the then derelict fort via these stairs – they didn't stay for long!

and so decided to clamber back into the darkness to continue his graffiti. However, the youth soon became lost in the labyrinth – every door he tried seemed to lead him further into the pitch-black fort – and after walking around in a daze for several minutes he gave up trying to find his way out and decided, bravely, to stay the night. However, when the teenager was discovered the next day by a volunteer, he was said to be so shaken that he refused to speak of what had happened the previous night.

On the Lower Gun Floor, Shane pointed out that weddings used to take place in the area. Apparently, during a ceremony one afternoon, something very peculiar happened. As the registrar was finalising the ceremony, a soldier in a red jacket emerged from nowhere and walked straight through the bride, groom and the rest of the congregation. The best man chased the figure as it strolled out of the tunnel, but when he met some of the re-enactment staff outside and enquired about the soldier in the red jacket, the staff replied that there was no one in a red jacket – all the staff were wearing blue jackets.

The incident was disturbing in a few ways. It's bad enough having a stranger interrupt the middle of your wedding, but it's even worse when you realise that the person was possibly a ghost. Worse still, it seems that the incident may have been a bad omen, as the couple, according to Shane, split up three months later!

As is the case in most reputedly haunted buildings, there is the usual slamming of doors and ghostly footsteps reported throughout the fort, but the Upper Gun Floor has one of the strangest ghost stories. Shane told me that during the Second World War a floor had been put in, quite high up in the room. When the trustees restored the fort, several people were standing on the

A while back a wedding ceremony was disrupted by the appearance of a phantom soldier.

It was in this room that a phantom floor appeared.

new floor when it suddenly vanished from under them. Seemingly, they were standing on an invisible platform. One of the witnesses claimed that when he looked down he could see several artillery men, as if he'd stepped back in time. The floor then flickered back into view. Since this incident, the floor has been demolished.

One of the most intriguing and longest lasting ghost stories connected to Fort Amherst also has ties to the nearby dockyard. Whilst no one is sure which location of the two is actually haunted, the story concerns a phantom drummer boy. According to Shane, many years ago a young drummer boy was accosted by two Royal Marines, who robbed and killed the child. The drummer boy was beheaded, his body was dumped on the marshes somewhere, and his head was entombed within his own drum before being buried in a chimney in the Royal Marine barracks. During the 1960s, when the barracks were demolished, it was alleged that the drum, containing a skull and a drum stick, were unearthed. The tale of the drummer boy appears to be nothing more than an oral yarn passed down through generations who, over time, have placed the ghost story in several locations, including the Great Lines which loom over Chatham – some say this is the location where the boy was killed. Despite embedding itself in local folklore, the case has been investigated in great depth by Pam Wood, who runs the Chatham Dockyard ghost tours, but I'll elaborate more on what really happened later.

And so, there we have it, Fort Amherst and its phantoms which, for several decades, have delighted tourists and ghost investigators alike. Whether such tantalising tales have factual origins we may never know, but one thing they do show is that a mere ghostly tale can exist on local lips for a long time, even if it is incorrect.

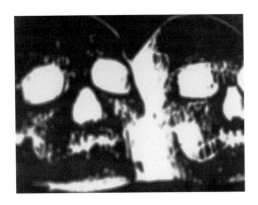

The phantom drummer boy's skull was allegedly found entombed within his own drum. (Image created by the author)

Here's one extra little tale for you, before we sign off from Amherst's anomalies. This story was reported by Mr John Blythe who, in contacting *Paranormal Magazine* in October 2010, spoke of a weird photograph that he had taken at the fort. The photograph, taken prior to a Haunted Weekend event, appeared to show a small, approximately 3ft tall, green-tinged figure standing behind the gate leading to the entrance tunnel of the fort. According to John, the creature 'was not seen with the naked eye', and he claimed that it had followed the group around the caves. My observations of the photograph are that it is a trick of the light, or a shadow, which looks to be something it isn't – and Shane, who gave me the tour, agreed.

I find myself looking at the many ghost hunts that have taken place at the fort, rather than the alleged ghosts, to analyse the haunted reputation of the fort. Many ghost-hunting groups have laid siege to the fort over the years, and this suggests to me that the human psyche holds more power than so-called paranormal entities. Many of the ghost stories have become distorted as they were passed from one generation to the next, so what a number of investigators are researching nowadays are in fact inaccurate stories. Strangely, some ghost-hunting groups claim to experience evidence of these legends despite the fact they are either nothing more than urban myth, or tales which were once based on actual events but which over time have been altered wildly. Sadly, whilst there are a few genuine investigators out there in the paranormal realm, many groups, promoters and alleged haunted locations exist for the sole purpose of making money. In 90 per cent of investigations it would seem that something 'paranormal' takes place, and such investigations have been plastered all over the internet. Amid the chaos of such investigations there are the usual, predictable reports of orbs, strange noises (clicking noises, creaks and things that go bump in the night – amidst the screaming audience!) and odd gusts of wind, coupled with the usual practices of table tipping and Ouija boards; which once again prove that the power of the mind is at work rather than an entity. Whilst some ghost investigations are put on to attract a vulnerable crowd, a small percentage of genuine encounters do appear to take place.

Susie Higgins and her partner Mark Gower investigated Fort Amherst a few years ago. Susie recounted their story to me in 2011:

Two incidents that stick in our minds took place at the Guard/Gate House. The building is on the far side of the grounds, opposite the tunnels. You descend down stone steps and under an arch which connects a similar building that has a dead-end road running through the middle. You then enter a two-storey, stone building which has a musty smell and large metal beds that protrude within the rooms. The ground floor has white curved ceilings with peeling paint. On the first floor are three two-bedded rooms which have big heavy damp mattresses stuffed with straw. Each room has an old fireplace with a fire basket and grate. It is a very foreboding building. On the first occasion, by torch light, we were led through with a group of other people, but we were at the back and as the people in front had moved along a lot quicker, we were left walking the first-floor corridor past the bedrooms. There was a distinct atmosphere of being followed and a feeling of dread, as you would feel if someone was walking close by behind you and was about to charge at you. This feeling became so intense and angry that we literally scrambled to get out of the corridor and up the stone steps outside to the grass level, and only then could we look behind us. This building has an alleged spirit the resident medium calls 'The Master', who allegedly attacks [the Medium] by dragging him out and slashing at his back. As a group we did witness him being 'attacked', which prompted two of the volunteer security staff to help him out of the building where he lifted his shirt and, for all to see, he had long fresh scratch marks on his back. There is definitely something festering in there but I would suggest it is just an angry spirit.

The second incident, a year later, we were back in the Guard/Gate House nearing the end of a paranormal investigation with Amherst's staff. This time each bedroom on the first floor individually held groups of people. In our room alone there were nine. A trigger alarm was set up in the corridor. Mark, my daughter Charlotte, and I were sitting on a low wooden bench with the beds to our left and other people, including a friend of ours named David, were sitting on them. In front of us was one of the volunteer helpers standing with his head just under a high level shelf. We were in semi-darkness, and I started to goad the nasty spirit that allegedly haunts the building. We could hear a knocking sound, similar to a piece of wood being hit against the wooden doors to each bedroom/bay. The atmosphere changed dramatically and several people commented on how uneasy they felt. Suddenly five of us witnessed a dark solid shadow form from the floor in front of the volunteer and slowly – this shadow became 6ft, then 7ft – grow up the wall to the ceiling. As soon as it did so, it shot out left and across two people sitting on a bed which made them jump and scream as they felt the pressure of it, then the shadow seemed to become black liquid off the bed, swoosh past us, which made us sit right back to let it pass, and then it disappeared through the closed door, setting the trigger alarm off. Some people were visibly shaken and I have to say it left us speechless. The volunteer who had worked the tunnels and the Guard/Gate House many a time was quite white with worry. Some people refused to continue within the building and asked to leave. That session came to an abrupt end.

Another set of unusual and possibly paranormal occurrences were related to me by a friend named Matt Newton, who said:

Around the late 1990s and early 2000s, Fort Amherst started to open their doors to the public for 'lock-ins' to experience their paranormal phenomena deep within the tunnels. This came off the back of *Most Haunted* etc., where people wanted a fright. There was a group of about thirty people all of varying ages and a friend of mine wished to experience the paranormal phenomena that Amherst had to offer, having been previously hyped in the local press.

We split into our groups, after being shown around to get a feel for the place, and were asked to then prepare ourselves for vigils lasting anything from 30–45 minutes, when we would then change

The network of tunnels beneath Fort Amherst has attracted thousands of ghost hunters over the years.

Fort Horsted

During the mid-nineteenth century, the UK defences were reviewed by a Royal Commission; Fort Horsted – situated off Primrose Close – was one of five forts built in Chatham, in response to the growing power and potential threat from the German enemy. It was built in 1880, supervised by the Royal Engineers. In 1976 a huge fire ravaged the fort. Nowadays, the fort is a venue for hire, with many rooms being used for a variety of things, including fashion shows and as business units.

There are a number of ghostly legends at the fort: one concerning a big, black shaggy dog said to roam around the creepy tunnels, another of a ghostly mother and daughter dressed in old-fashioned attire, and the spirit of a little girl whose voice has been heard on occasion by visitors. It's no surprise that several ghost hunts have taken place at Fort Horsted. One of the most productive was conducted by Missy Lindley and her mother Corriene on the evening of 30 April 2010. More than twenty people had joined the ghost hunt, which took them into the Counterscarp Gallery, also known as the 'Graffiti Room'. The group, who were all men, were unaware that Missy and Corriene were recording the hunt on a Dictaphone, and the night was also filmed using a night-vision camera. Whilst in the room, one of the men made a lewd comment about a drawing on the wall. When Missy and her mum played the video back, at this exact point there is a very eerie voice of a man who seems to say something along the lines of, 'Saw some people', which is then followed by what seems to be a child – a young boy – who says, 'It's a Nazi (or 'nasty') bomb.' As this is heard, there appears to be a booming sound in the background, coming from outside and above as if bombs

positions so that everyone experienced the same area and possible encounter. We were not told of any of the potential inhabitants, for fear of creating hysteria.

On walking around through the various tunnels, having taken our turn, and having changed to the next location, I saw what could only be described as an explosion of blue sparks, like a mini blue fireworks display at the base of the stairs, which caught my eye in a split second. I immediately asked my friend if he saw the same display, which he had not, and with this striking image stuck in my mind [I] continued to be excited at the thought of seeing other paranormal events.

Upon returning to the central area where we would meet for soup and heat, we were asked if anyone had seen anything. Keen to inform them of my experience, I relayed this to them and was told that what I saw had been a common experience, where some people had seen the image of a Second World War officer standing in full uniform at the bottom of the stairs with a briefcase. Most people that had seen the full manifestation of the officer had started to see blue sparks before he had appeared at the location seen by me.

Fort Horsted.

are falling – this then fades and the child's voice is cut off by what sounds like a 'shh shh', or snigger from the unseen male. Bizarrely, none of this was heard on the actual investigation. I have watched this video, thanks to Missy and Corriene, and it sent shivers up my spine, especially the child's voice which is loud and clear.

Missy, in conversation, also mentioned another investigation at the fort, stating:

Mum was asking spirits present to give her a sign … suddenly there's a loud screeching which cuts across the tape, and when enhanced sounds like a table being scraped across the ground. The magazine we were in at the time was completely empty and then after the screech there are two whispering voices, which very slowly state, 'It's dark,' the other, very quickly comments, 'Careful!'

Is this a photograph of a ghost taken at Fort Horsted?
(Picture courtesy of Missy Lindley and Corriene Vickers)

Later in the evening Missy recalled how a male voice, with a slight American accent, said 'Okay' after she asked the spirits for a sign. Two female voices – albeit moaning ones – were also heard. Missy also recounted how two photographs were taken on the investigation, one showing a weird shadow (which hadn't been cast by anyone present), which had disappeared by the time the next photograph was taken.

Fort Luton

Fort Luton was built in the late 1800s. During the First World War it was used as a barracks and training base for troops being sent to France. In the Second World War the fort was used as an anti-aircraft base. It stood derelict from 1947 until the early 1990s, when it operated as a museum. The fort, which overlooks the Luton valley, is situated on Magpie Hall Road. It is now derelict and fenced off from the public.

During the 1960s a group of young men were hanging around the old fort when they were stunned by the apparition of several 'stretcher bearers', who were hurriedly walking over the old drawbridge that crossed the dirt moat. The figures appeared to be shimmering. Shortly afterwards a local man, who owned the nearby garage, said he'd seen the same phantoms carrying a stretcher. Ghostly soldiers have also been observed scrambling around the ruins.

Fort Darland

Situated on the Chatham–Gillingham border, Fort Darland (which was demolished in the 1960s) was the last of the Chatham forts to be built (construction was completed in 1899).

A brief ghost story of this fort is mentioned on the Medway Memories website. Website owner Steve Rayner writes:

My correspondent – who asks not to be named – bought a bungalow in Montrose Avenue in the early 1970s and discovered that adjoining homes had been built over Darland's moat. He writes: 'We lived happily enough there although an odd incident right at the start caused us some concern. There were two extremely large bedrooms and we decided to have one of them divided. Our three-year-old son slept in the bedroom to be altered and within a couple of days of moving in, a doorway for the third bedroom had been cut out and the frame of the internal dividing wall was in place. About 10 p.m. I heard our young son screaming in terror. I flew up the stairs and found him sitting bolt upright in his bed. He described an old man walking past his bed and told me that he heard him go into the bathroom. From his description the figure was in some sort of uniform and was carrying a rifle. I looked all over but could see nothing. I sat with him until he went back to sleep and then went downstairs but sat with the lounge door wide open. The least sound made me jumpy, but the rest of the night passed uneventfully.'

'Next day, my son made no reference to what had happened until I was reading him a bedtime story. Then he said, "Daddy – don't let that thing come in my room tonight."'

'Fortunately there were no further incidents until years later. I came in late one night after watching the Gills in an evening kick-off and my wife told me as I was closing the front door that she had seen an old man in Army-style uniform standing on the stairs – or rather the upper part of him.'

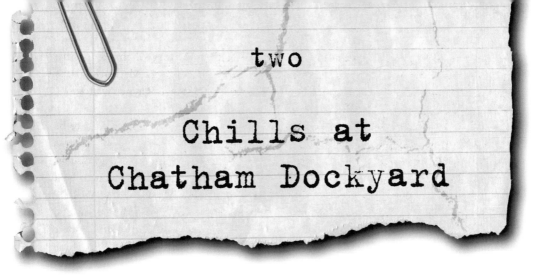

two

Chills at Chatham Dockyard

I knew now that I had entered some hitherto unimagined – indeed, unbelieved-in – realm of consciousness, that coming to this place had already changed me and that there was no going back.

Susan Hill – *The Woman in Black*

When I was a child (during the late 1970s and early '80s) my dad and granddad worked at Chatham's Historic Dockyard – now an 80-acre site dotted by historic warships, museum galleries and old buildings. One story that always stuck in my mind concerned my dad, Ron. One night, after working his shift – he was employed to water-blast the inside of submarines before painting them – he was in the rest room (which used to overlook Number One basin), 'getting his head down'. The door to the room was ajar, and yet through the crack my dad could see the figure of an old man peering back at him. The man wore similar overalls, but my dad was not familiar with the chap as being on the same shift, and he sensed that there was something unusual and 'old fashioned'

about him. This was confirmed when the man very slowly began to fade away until he no longer stood in the doorway. Another employee in the room saw my dad slowly sit up and gaze towards the door, but they did not discuss what he had seen. My dad felt no malevolence from the phantom and the next day, whilst making a cup of tea, my dad was approached by the other worker who said that he had also seen the figure in the overalls vanish into thin air.

I have always enjoyed this story, and only a few years ago I was told of an even weirder encounter involving a couple of gentlemen who were working in an outside room at the Dockyard. I don't recall what their job entailed, but one afternoon they'd been asked to clear out one of the rooms which was packed full of old junk and had become choked with weeds. Upon entering the room both men shouted in horror as a black, phantasmal creature came rushing past them out of the door. One of the witnesses stated categorically that the 'animal' had not been a domestic cat or fox, but something far larger which moved at lightning speed.

Main gate of Chatham Historic Dockyard, on Dock Road.

Chatham Dockyard and Fort Amherst are situated within close proximity of one another.

During certain months of the year, ghost tours are conducted throughout the most haunted parts of Chatham's Dockyard. The two stories you've just read are probably just a small percentage of the many which have been missed by the Dockyard staff. But this is understandable, because as you are about to read, Chatham's Dockyard harbours an overwhelming gaggle of ghosts and ghouls, and so cataloguing every sinister tale is nigh on impossible.

The *Medway Messenger* of 2 February 2004 ran, 'Getting into the spirit', with Peter Cook reporting:

Spooks and spectres in Chatham's Historic Dockyard will have the tables turned on them, starting next month. They're bracing themselves to be haunted by people who sign up for ghost walks. The Dockyard has the fifth most haunted house in Britain within its walls – Commissioner's House. The walks are helping to reveal even more ghosts.

'I was giving a talk in the Commissioner's Garden when I noticed two women looking straight past me,' said a duty manager who conducted the walks wearing eighteenth-century costume.

'They said they could see a young girl in her early teens standing on the lawn. Apparently they could smell horses. But when the girl disappeared through the gate out of the garden, the smell disappeared. That was a new one on me. Presumably she was a stable girl from the days when horses were kept here. On another occasion I came into the garden ahead of the tour. The door was shut though I knew I had opened it earlier. While I was standing in the garden the door slammed shut. I opened it and looked around but there was nobody there. This happened three or four times.'

In 1961, one of the first ever ghost hunts was conducted at the Drill Hall, Dock Road. It was reported in the *Chatham Standard* of 31 October, under the heading, 'It's Hallowe'en and we're ghost huntin' tonight!', accompanied by a photograph of members of the Medway Caledonian Society celebrating the occasion.

The *Chatham, Rochester & Gillingham News* of 10 November 1950 featured an interesting article – to confirm the ghostly reputation of the Dockyard – by Frederick Sanders which I produce here in its entirety. Frederick Sanders, often investigated and wrote of local ghostly happenings. Under the heading 'Phantom squad's midnight parade', Sanders reported:

The last men of the Royal Marines (Chatham Division) had hardly moved out of the Royal Marine barracks in Dock Road, before the 'Spirit of the Past' descended upon those buildings, and took ghostly charge of the tree-lined parade-ground and the clock tower. In other words, the barracks became haunted as from midnight on Friday 20 October.

As the clock struck the witching hour something uncanny came into being. Hardly had the last stroke died away before the light in the tower flickered and went out; the mechanism ceased to function and the hands remained stationary. During the following week several attempts were made to get the clock to go. For a few hours it worked well, and then at various times, from 5.25 p.m. to 8.45 p.m., it would immobilise itself. There is nothing mechanically wrong with the ex-Royal Marine barracks' clock. The formerly illuminated clock tower has become haunted!

The Clock Tower in the Dockyard was, according to researcher Frederick Sanders, haunted.

Then, under the heading, 'The Ghost of Mental Projection', Sanders continues:

Is there some strange psychic force, some weird form of reciprocal-spherical wave-activity set up within the now haunted tower that, though it does not stop the clock from working short periods, yet has power enough, when it has reached a certain pitch, to halt the mechanism? A force built up by the accumulation of recent mass thought 'forms' or waves of kindred oscillations by men of the Royal Marines, still serving, also all those ex-Royals who rest 'on arms reversed', who have thought, and in their hearts grieved at the disestablishment of the R.M. Depot set up something akin to a 'radio-active' phenomenon based on massed thought-projection upon one definite place: in this instance the

The Clock Tower, formerly the Royal Naval storehouse.

R.M. Barracks. It is possible that such phenomena could exist there, and would persist for a considerable period of time. Nothing that exists can ever be destroyed, though it can be altered. Thought is one of the newest of created things, as it only made its appearance on glimmerings of reason in the minds of pre-historic man. Thought, no doubt, has a chemical basis from which it activates, and if so, then thought made mentally conscious prior to its being made known to speech, music, or the brush or pen, must therefore continue to exist.

Mr Sanders was known for his rather heavy-going prose, but it is worth sticking with his tale. He continues under the title 'Parade of the spectral Royals':

From midnight on 23 October, and each midnight following up to that of the 27th, I kept watch in and around the haunted area. It was not until the night of Friday 27th, that anything untoward happened except for the continual stopping of the barrack clock. I had strolled away from the barracks and was turning round at the top of the hill leading down to Pembroke Naval Barracks, when a hatless and very distraught young sailor stopped me and asked for a match to light a cigarette he held in trembling fingers. I remarked to him that he seemed in a rather rough state, and jocularly referred his 'all shot to pieces' attitude to 'Wine, Women and Song'. He pulled himself together a bit, tried to find his cap and made a one-handed attempt to readjust his white silk muffler. All the time he kept looking around in a frightened way, and glancing quickly every few seconds over his shoulder. It was not 'Wine, Women and Song' he explained, but ghosts!

As he was coming past the deserted R.M. Barracks he had stopped to look through the gates to see what the time was by the clock in the tower, when suddenly he caught the far away tread of marching feet. Nearer and nearer came the steady tramp, tramp, tramping. Then, before his startled gaze appeared the band of the Royal Marines followed by a standard bearer, behind whom marched a squad of marines with fixed bayonets! I brought to the notice of the gentleman-in-blue that if the squad was really a 'ghost squad' he would not have heard them, but only seen them. He shakingly told me that was perhaps what I thought, but he'd seen them and heard them, and he knew they were ghosts of Royal Marines because though the band was playing, no martial music filled the midnight air! Mumbling his thanks for the light, he lurched away, and with a sharp, weird cry ran down the hill towards HMS *Pembroke*.

Sanders concluded his article under the final heading of 'Voice of the leaves', stating:

As I have had several encounters with naval 'ghosts' at St Mary's Barracks, and at the old Naval Camp at 'Laughing Water', Cobham, I hurried back to the R.M. Depot to see the 'ghost squad' at work, and to try to fathom out the mystery of the haunted square. I walked along as far as St Mary's Church, then about-faced and strolled back to the Depot, passing the first gloomy gate where once-friendly sentries had stood and from the lighted windows of the guard room cheerful light had shone forth into the night. Then I reached the main entrance and stopped, and gazed through the iron-work of the gates across to the shrouded clock tower with its light-less clock. It was not long before I heard a strange sound – a familiar one to me –

the far away sibilant noise of regimented marching feet! Steadily they came, and stronger, like a ghostly 'Boys of the Old Brigade'. Then suddenly came a gust of wind and a great gout of crisp leaves raced over the parade before me. The breeze died, and the leaves of autumn scurried to rest. There was nothing to see. All was silence. The intermittent night breezes moving the great quantities of brown and gold leaves about the square had caused the sailor to 'see' the Phantom Parade! He had heard what I heard, and noted the peculiar sounds of marching men. His imagination had done the rest, and he really did 'see', mentally, a very vivid picture that had been unconsciously conjured up. The proof of this is that he heard the marching feet because he had heard the movements of the leaves, but he did not hear the band, because there was no sound band-like enough to couple up with this mental projection of the 'Midnight Royals'.

Sanders' rather confusing explanation for the sailor's experience was typical of how, during the 1940s and '50s, he led the reader on a complex and at times meandering mystery tour before explaining it all away as natural phenomena. Of course, the rush of autumn leaves cannot explain every ghostly encounter that has taken place at Chatham Dockyard.

Peter Underwood, in his book *Ghosts of Kent*, quotes Samuel Pepys, who, on his 1661 visit to the Dockyard, commented:

Then to the Hill House at Chatham, where I never was before, and I found a pretty pleasant house, and am pleased with the armes that hang up there. Here we supped very merry, and late to bed; Sir William telling me that old Edgebarrow, his predecessor, did die and walk in my

chamber did make me somewhat afraid, but not so much as for mirth's sake I did seem. So to bed in the Treasurer's chamber. Lay and slept till three in the morning, and then waking and by the light of the moon I saw my pillow (which overnight I flung from me) stand upright, but not bethinking myself that it might be I was a little afraid, but sleep overcame all, and so lay till nigh morning, at which time I had a candle brought me, and a good fire made, and in general it was a great pleasure all the time I staid here to see how I am respected and honoured by all people … [sic]

Underwood goes on to speak of the ghostly sound of limping footsteps, and the 'tapping of a crutch or wooden leg' in the vicinity of St Mary's Barracks. Legend has it that the ghost is that of an ex-serviceman who was shot after being mistaken for an intruder. Underwood states that, 'The sounds have most frequently been reported during the Middle watch, midnight to 4 a.m., when, it might be thought, the night is at its darkest, shadows can easily assume physical forms and mistakes can easily happen.'

Although the ghost may be nothing more than the product of an overactive imagination, it has acquired a name over the years – Peg-Leg Jack. He has also been heard towards Room 34 of Cumberland Block, said to be the oldest part of the barracks. Despite Sanders and Underwood's belief that the 'ghosts' are nothing more than misidentification, there is said to exist an official log of a ghost sighting. It was recorded as 'Ghost reported seen during Middle watch', in the logbook of the then duty officer. However, Pam Wood discounts the haunting as being related to the Dockyard gates, and claims that if such a character does haunt the Dockyard then it would be in the vicinity of Greenwich

*Arthur Prosser's sketch for the **Evening Post**, regarding the peg-legged phantom.*

University – formerly HMS *Pembroke* – where in the past a report was made regarding someone hearing the wooden leg of an unseen individual.

According to Arthur Prosser, who sketched a number of ghosts for the *Evening Post*, the peg-legged phantom was last seen in 1949. Prosser writes, 'It is believed the sailor was murdered by escaping French prisoners.'

Strangely, author Rupert Matthews, in his book *Ghost Hunter Walks in Kent,* contradicts the legend somewhat, claiming that the sounds of the limping ghost are heard outside the main gate. Matthews also writes that the sounds suggest the ghost is of a man who 'uses a wooden walking stick every other step'.

An obscure and brief article, pertaining to the peg-legged ghost, appeared in the *Edmonton Journal*, an American newspaper of all places, on 14 February 1949, with the heading, 'Ghost of old sailor seeks haunted house':

> Chatham – Kent – England – The ghost of a one-legged sailor who fought in the Battle of Trafalgar is house-hunting. Up to now he has haunted St Mary's naval barracks here, oldest barrack block in the United Kingdom, but the building has been scheduled for demolition. The ghost sports a tarred pigtail and a bandana kerchief. Many claim to have seen him around the barracks in recent years.

The *Chatham Standard*, of 8 November 1950, recorded that some 521 skulls and other remains had been buried beside

On the sign:

Commissioner's House (1703)

*Myself nor my family doe lie is ye old house
for fear of its falling upon our heads
Commissioner St Lo, July 5, 1703*

Materials and workmanship, what cost?
Nine hundred pounds and more. Bring bricklayers,
bring bricks and lyme. No time is to be lost

The Commissioner's House, home to several spirits since 1704. (Despite what this sign says!)

St George's Church at the naval barracks. And, as mentioned in the introduction, Anglo-Saxon remains were discovered by Royal Engineers at the Kitchener Barracks.

Commissioner's House, originally constructed in 1640 for Phineas Pett (the first Resident Commissioner) was demolished in 1703 and rebuilt in 1704. It existed as a grand residence, and, according to Pam Wood:

> The house is the oldest, and probably the most attractive, naval building to survive intact in Britain today. The building remains relatively unchanged since it was built with a few additions to the interior between 1770 and 1780 and the servants' quarters that were added to the south of the building at the same time. The main staircase has a large ceiling painting depicting an assembly of gods … the garden can be viewed by entering through either of the garden gates. The terraces were established before the present house was constructed, [and] the lower terrace was one of the very first Italianate water gardens in Britain when laid out.

John Evelyn wrote of it 'resembling some fine villa about Rome'.

The gardens contain a mulberry tree said to be over four centuries old and also an eighteenth-century ice house. Over the last few centuries the gardens have experienced several positive changes, and they are now open to the public.

Alongside its intriguing history, Commissioner's House is also rumoured to be extremely haunted. According to Pam:

Paranormal activity has taken place during several ghost tours of Commissioner's House

During the ghost tours that took place throughout the house on 5/6 December 2006, people within the tour groups claimed to have seen children on the stairs. During the two-day event the descriptions of the children were consistent, three boys and two girls. Two of the boys are quite small, possibly between the ages of three to five years, the other one may be as old as seven. The girls' ages are between seven and eleven.

Pam also wrote that in a room known as The Revenge (the rooms are named after warships) there is reputedly the wandering spirit of a young woman. The temperature is said to drop suddenly when the spectre is present. Those who have seen the ghost claim that she sits in the alcove window on the right of the room, and an overwhelming sadness has been experienced by those sensitive to the spirit's presence. An adjacent room has also experienced ghostly activity. A couple that used to reside at the house said that their son, whilst playing in the room, reported sudden drops in temperature and banging noises. They also mentioned that their son had spoken of being in the company of a spectral woman. Another room said to be haunted within the house is the Sunne Room. During the 1990s a guest attending a wedding reception claimed they'd seen the phantom of a woman in a long dress. The ghost crossed the room from the direction of the fireplace and headed towards the servants' stairs. Interestingly, these stairs harbour a legend concerning a young woman who, many years ago, was said to have taken her own life by hanging. Pam believes the ghost story is a classic tale which has been passed down through several generations, and it often makes reference to the young woman discovering, while with child, that her boyfriend, away at sea, has lost his life. Fearing that she'd become an outcast for having a fatherless child, the forlorn woman takes to the top of the stairs and days later is found dead, hanging from her makeshift noose. Since this dreadful event, the stairs are rumoured to be haunted by the girl. Those who sense her presence and the feeling of overwhelming sadness, also report a drop in temperature.

One of the most consistent reports of paranormal activity centred on the Nursery Room in the attic – and let's face it, attics are always considered spooky places! Pam told me how over two nights there were fourteen tours, comprising a total of 330 people, and in each group at least one person described seeing a blonde-haired girl in a white dress, aged between seven and nine.

Whilst in the Commissioner's Garden a witness experienced one of the Dockyard's most impressive ghost sightings. One night in 2004 a woman named Sammy, one of the guides on the ghost tour, and her partner Ian, were videoing the tour. Whilst looking through the viewfinder in the direction of the back of the house, Ian was shocked to see a ghostly figure looking back from one of the windows. Ian peered over his camera lens and then back through the viewfinder. Clicking the camera on to night-vision mode, Ian could clearly see the figure of a man wearing a jacket with double buttons. When Ian stared more intently, he realised that in front of the man was a second figure

The garden of Commissioner's House.

– a woman – sitting in a chair, and both of these apparitions were staring directly back at him!

In 1957, a Laurie Debona worked at Chatham Dockyard. Laurie was employed as an assistant chef to the admiral superintendent. He was part of a team of five or six whose jobs were simple – to keep the senior officers happy. The small group of staff resided in an annexe which was connected to the Admiral Superintendent's eighteenth-century quarters – Commissioner's House. One of Laurie's colleagues was a man named Sharkey Ward. One dark October night he had a frightful encounter that he would never forget. At the end of each evening, Sharkey's job was to stoke the boilers for the central heating, which meant a trip to the basement of the house. Just before 10.30 p.m., with the rest of the staff tucked up in bed, Sharkey conducted his rounds which took him to the outside greenhouse boiler. Suddenly, Sharkey heard voices. Immediately, thinking there were intruders present, Sharkey crept along the back of the house towards where he could hear voices coming from the direction of the lawn. Oddly, there was an eerie glow coming from the lawn, and it was then that Sharkey observed two men. They appeared to be Cavaliers and they were shouting at one another. Sharkey decided that the best thing to do was to approach them and defuse the row, but as he headed towards the two gentlemen they completely vanished. With that Sharkey fled in terror, rushing back to the living quarters to tell his comrades of his encounter.

Many years later, in speaking to the local *Kent Messenger*, Laurie Debona recalled:

Sharkey was shaking. We didn't know what to do with him. Then one of the lads got him a beer and shoved it in his hand. He could hardly hold his beer, he was shaking so much. It took him a good half-hour to sort himself out and start to tell us what he had seen. He was genuinely shocked.

Although Laurie never saw a ghost at the Dockyard, he was spooked by the fact that the two dachshund dogs, which belonged to the Admiral's wife, always refused to walk across the lawn. Laurie also remembered a few other ghostly tales:

There had been tales of a ghost in the house, an old lady dressed in black up in the attic. The stewards reckoned every time they went to get linen out of the cupboard, she was behind them. They could feel a cold presence. And we knew about the seventeenth-century drummer boy who was said to have hanged himself on St Mary's Island. Every November, he's supposed to walk the length of the barracks playing his drum.

Matt Newton (*see* Chapter One) also spoke of peculiar events concerning Commissioner's House.

During the late 1990s Chatham Historic Dockyard produced various tickets for groups to come and experience an evening within Commissioner's House. Due to a change of ownership, there was a short window to take a tour inside the house before new ownership and also to participate in an evening with a group of mediums holding séances around the house. There were about twenty-five or so people and it was during December, as mulled wine and mince pies were prepared for our arrival. We were split into two groups and taken on a tour of the house and gardens. Leading us were two guides who had a good knowledge of the building and some of its ethereal inhabitants. The male guide was dressed in period costume. It was said he had been personally contacted by one of the resident ghosts, who had allegedly hanged herself in one of the large Georgian-style windows that fronts the river.

As we were in the second group we waited and chatted with other tour members, [when] we suddenly heard an almighty scream from the attic space and we all jumped up wondering if it was a staged event, only to find that when looking up the stairs there was a middle-aged lady absolutely petrified running down the stairs with someone from the group chasing her. She fled the doors and ran into the darkness of the Dockyard never seen to return that evening.

After much disruption we were told that the attic space was rife with spirits of children. It was alleged that the lady was touched on the leg by a child spirit, which sent her running. The experience only served to pump more adrenaline and we were hoping to experience great things in the attic space. Unfortunately, the events that took place within our group were not successful, but we were told that there would be a placing of trigger objects in the loft space throughout the course of the night and we were welcome to contact them in the morning to find out if anything had happened. As this was all relatively new, I doubt there were sufficient insurances in place to cover the group should anything happen during the middle of the night.

We went home slightly disappointed that nothing [had] happened to us, but after contacting the group the next day we were told that items such as a child's trolley with letter blocks in one corner of the attic rooms had been set up, and also the mantelpiece had been dusted with talcum powder and the door locked. When tour guides returned the next day and unlocked the room they found that the child's trolley had been rolled to the centre of the floor, the blocks had tumbled from the stack and on the mantelpiece there were child's fingerprints in the talc, smudged due to the height of the of mantel. This confirmed to the group of investigators that night that the children were active, but were also shy and wished to play. The children are apparently quite a regular sight at the house.

(Author's note: This has never been verified. In October 2011 Pam Wood stated that the attic door had never been locked and it was unlikely that such an experiment had been carried out.)

Paranormal Magazine reported on more maritime manifestations, this time from 2007:

Mick, a member of the local Chatham Historical Society, and his dog Ben, were staying at the Historic Dockyard at Chatham in their camper van. During the evening, Ben suddenly started to growl at something or someone outside. Unusual behaviour for such a mild-mannered dog thought Mick, trying to calm him.

He looked out of the window but could see nothing in the enveloping blackness that might have caused his dog to behave in such a manner. Mick was uneasy. He looked outside but nobody was there. He went back into the van and Ben started growling again, the hackles rising on the back of his neck. Then Mick saw something that chilled him to the bone.

An inexplicable mist was appearing and disappearing on the side window as if someone were breathing on it. Mick went back outside. Still there was not a living soul in sight. It struck him that the mist on the glass was about the height of a young child. Perhaps the cause of it was the mischievous ghostly children who roam around the Dockyard playing their tricks?

On 18 February 2010, the *Telegraph* ran an article on Fred Cordier, Master Ropemaker at the Dockyard. According to the newspaper, the Ropery '... built in 1790 ... was the longest brick building in the world'.

At the time of the article, Fred had worked at the Ropery for almost fifty years. With rope still in high demand at the time, Fred's employment was a job for life, and during his time at the Dockyard he had experienced a few ghosts, according to the newspaper.

'I've seen a few ghosts. Sometimes it can feel a bit funny, especially when you are switching the lights off at night. Each light has to be switched off individually and, as you are walking along, you hear people behind you.'

The Ropery is also said to be haunted by a handful of 'Bobbin Boys', children dressed in tatty attire dating back a couple of centuries or more. In September 2011, one of the security guards at the Dockyard mentioned that, whilst working late one night in the Ropery, he'd been spooked by the sound of footsteps when there was no one else in the building. The Smithery also has a couple of intriguing stories attached to it. During the nineteenth century a boiler exploded in

The haunted Ropery.

The Smithery.

the area, killing several people; this was the second tragedy connected to the location. During the Second World War an enemy plane dropped a bomb in the area, resulting in several deaths. The area of the new gallery at the Smithery is haunted by an unseen presence that, on one occasion, pushed a cleaner who was working there. According to Pam Wood, the woman resigned from her post, so unnerved was she by the encounter. During a ghost investigation on 12 May 2011, a strange ball of light was observed in the area too.

Despite this bewildering array of ghostly tales, Pam believes that the most haunted parts of the Dockyard are the Mast House and the Mould Loft. Members of the public, whilst visiting the Mast House, have reported excruciating pains in their heads – when standing almost on the exact spot where an alleged murder took place in 1875. Whilst researching a paper, Pam discovered that at approximately 3 p.m. on 16 April 1875 two men were working on a mast. One of the men was shaping the timbers, whilst the other was watching him; the onlooker was in possession of an adze – a pickaxe-type tool. It was alleged that the silent man struck the other man across the head, one fatal blow resulting in death. The allegedly murdered man – James Catt, from Gillingham – gasped his final breath and lay in a pool of blood. His supposed murderer, George Blampied, a neighbour, and so-called friend of Catt, strolled casually away from the limp body. Other workers heard the final screams of Catt and ran to his aid, and when they approached Blampied, he said, 'Jemmy's killed himself with my adze.'

The Mast House, believed by Pam Wood to be one of the Dockyard's most haunted locations.

Blampied, despite stating that Catt had committed suicide, was taken into custody by the Dockyard police and was considered not of sound mind. according to Pam in her research, '… it would appear that some few years before he had been confined in Barming Asylum near Maidstone'. Pam added:

He re-entered Chatham Dockyard about two years previous, and he had worked in the yard uninterrupted since then. On being taken into custody, he made no protest and appeared to be the least affected by what had occurred. It was remarked at the time that his bearing was scarcely that of a sane man, under the awful circumstances. The Dockyard police established that he was engaged upon the *Alexandra* until recently, but the noise affected his head and

he was placed in the Mast House as it is very quiet there. Although it was known that he had been in the asylum and that his head had again begun to be affected, he was not thought to be dangerous.

Pam's in-depth investigations revealed that the alleged murdered man, James Catt, 'was removed to the Dead-house at Melville Hospital, to await an inquest. Catt's funeral took place on 25 April 1875'. Pam concluded, 'The Mast House, the place where the frightful affair took place, was enclosed and nothing touched until after it had been viewed by the jury …'

George Blampied, proven to be criminally insane, spent the rest of his life at Broadmoor Hospital.

One wonders if such a tragic event has embedded itself into the framework of the

In 1875 an alleged murder took place in the Mast House involving James Catt and George Blampied, who were shaping timbers.

Mast House, and occasionally, those susceptible to unexplained phenomena, are bestowed with that searing pain – a ghostly re-enactment of that terrible murder?

Shadowy figures seen out of the corner of the eye, eerie reflections in the glass, and the scent of old-fashioned perfume – sometimes lavender, on other occasions the scent of crushed roses – are just some of the peculiar instances of strangeness which have taken place in the Mast House. One Halloween, during a ghost investigation, questions were aimed at an unseen spirit which replied with a series of knocks, and a medium picked up the presence of a man known to staff as Abel, who, during the seventeenth century, was a seaman. He is said to loiter in the area of the loft, which, constructed in 1753, was made of old ship timbers. In the same area there were also noises which originally suggested

a crying baby, but on further investigation they sounded more like a small monkey. This would make sense as it is quite possible that Abel, the seaman, had a pet monkey on-board his ship, the timbers of which eventually ended up being used for the frame of the loft.

When I spoke to Pam in September 2011, she managed to clear up the mystery of the drummer boy ghost (*see* Chapter One). According to Pam, the drummer boy legend is a 'Dockyard story of oral history', a tale passed down through many generations, especially in Royal Marine circles. Although she couldn't tie the haunting to one particular spot, she has delved into the facts behind the crime which spawned the ghost story.

On Sunday 30 June 1872 at 11.30 a.m., teenager George Thomas Stock – a drum-

The phantom drummer boy. (Illustration by Simon Wyatt)

mer boy – had his throat slit in the Royal Marine library (now the Gun Wharf which houses the council offices) by veteran Royal Marine James Tooth. Tooth, aged forty, a private of the 4th Company Royal Marines, who had been transferred from Woolwich to Chatham, had apparently lent money to the boy. At the time, this was considered a violation of the regulations, and eventually, during a fit of rage – fuelled by a severe reprimand from senior officers and possibly a beer or two – he killed the youngster, albeit in a carefully planned manner. When no one else was present in the library, Tooth crept up behind the youth whilst he was reading a copy of the *London Journal*, and slit his throat from ear to ear, severing the windpipe.

Tooth fled the scene and Stock staggered down the stairs and collapsed on the parade ground, where he was aided by other drummer boys. But within the hour, the teenager had died. Immediately

afterwards a search of the barracks was conducted, the authorities looking for someone spattered with blood. Tooth was apprehended at the Royal Marine barracks – found with blood on his hands. Tooth denied killing the boy, but after several interrogations he finally confessed. He was sentenced to death and executed on 13 August 1872, but during the time he spent at Maidstone Gaol he spoke about being haunted by the ghost of the drummer boy.

Bill Bishop's article for *True Crime* states that, with regards to Tooth, he 'must have realised that in fraternising with an adolescent in public his intentions would then, as now, have been highly suspect.' He explains that Tooth and Stock had returned from a church service and had gone into the canteen, where Tooth had barged his way to the bar and ordered himself a beer whilst the drummer boy had a shandy. To escape the noise, Stock had slipped off to the reading room in the library. The sergeant's wife, Ellen Plumstead, saw Stock go to the library and then watched as Tooth followed shortly afterwards. Plumstead then heard frightful screams and along with a Private Dare saw Stock stumble down the stairs clutching his throat. According to Bishop, Dare ran to Stock's aid as Tooth marched from the room. Despite gurgling blood, George Stock managed to point an accusing finger towards Tooth. Two passing marines were ordered by a Corporal Cheshire to take Stock to Melville Barracks Hospital while Cheshire, accompanied by another marine, went in search of Tooth. Bishop comments that when the men could not find their elusive quarry they informed a Lieutenant Price of the incident. Dare identified Tooth as the offender and, when questioned, according to Bishop, Tooth was quite arrogant and eventually removed a cut-throat razor from his pocket and cast it to the floor, implying that it was the weapon he used to commit the crime.

Bishop also mentions that the inquest on Stock was held at the Queens Head Inn, Brompton, on 20 July 1872, where Tooth pleaded guilty. Bishop does not mention Tooth being literally haunted by the drummer boy, but instead concludes that whilst staying at Chatham Police Station, the few days before being taken to Maidstone Gaol, Tooth had been so tormented by what he'd done that every time he closed his eyes all he saw was the face of George Stock.

I asked Pam if there'd been any recent sightings of the ghostly boy, but he doesn't seem to have put in an appearance. There is one story which seems to connect the legend with the actual Dockyard, and it may have involved the vicar of St Mary's Church (the church being a short distance from the Dockyard). One night, whilst entering the sentry gate, the vicar claimed to have seen the phantom boy. No date can be confirmed for the sighting. One thing that can be suspected regarding the drummer boy story is that the details, concerning a killing on the marsh, and the skull found in a drum, are more than likely nothing more than myth – or a campfire tale which has become rooted in local history.

In his book *Ghost Hunter Walks in Kent*, Rupert Matthews states that another ghost of the Dockyard is that of Admiral Horatio Nelson, who was killed in the 1805 Battle of Trafalgar. Why on earth Admiral Nelson should still haunt Chatham Dockyard no one knows, or can verify, but according to Matthews:

Nelson was shot down in the moment of victory, his body being brought back to Britain for a state funeral at St Paul's, London. ... Soon afterwards, Nelson's ghost began to walk in the Dockyards of Chatham. Strangely, the phantom does not appear as Nelson did when he died, but as a young man complete with both arms and both eyes.

(Author's note: Nelson lost his right arm in battle in 1797, and three years previous lost sight in his right eye.)

Pam Wood dismisses this haunting as mere legend, as there do not seem to be any sightings of Nelson within the vicinity of the Dockyard. Once again this is a case of inaccurate legends being passed down through generations.

In 2004 the team from the popular television show *Most Haunted* visited Chatham Dockyard. Members of the team – including presenter Yvette Fielding, historian Richard Felix, researcher Phil Whyman, and medium Derek Acorah – staked out different areas of the location. They were accompanied by a duty manager and tour host. The duty manager commented that the most likely place for something unusual to happen was Commissioner's House. The tour host mentioned that in the past she'd been pushed, and had been rocked backwards and forwards by an invisible presence; she had also picked up extreme cold spots. Whilst in Commissioner's House, Derek Acorah sensed a female energy – a 'bossy' woman of supervisory status who had passed around 1956. These details could not be verified. Derek believed the female was named Lizzie, and in the attic area he picked up an accompanying male spirit. Both of these spirits were perceived as hostile and Derek stated that the female phantom had been responsible for looking after children in the nursery but had mistreated, and even possibly killed some of the children. There were no records of this ever occurring, and the name of Leonard for the male figure could not be confirmed either. Derek also mentioned that the male figure was responsible for some of the strange noises that had been heard, such as a screeching sound as if something was being dragged across the floor. The team conducted a séance in the attic and Derek claimed to be possessed by a nine-year-old child named Barney Little. The child entity alleged that he'd been whipped by the woman named Lizzie. It was then that Derek became possessed by Lizzie, but no details of note were forthcoming.

In the Joiners Shop a strong feeling of foreboding came over Yvette and Derek. Derek claimed that a male 'nuisance spirit' was in the vicinity and that this entity may have been a soldier who had killed someone. The duty manager claimed that something had whistled past his head, clipping his ear, and then Derek Acorah – claiming to be possessed by the spirit of a soldier named Richard Neville – collapsed on the floor. The team were also spooked by unusual gusts of wind – the vigil was conducted on a very chilly, blustery night – and several banging noises, although most of these were explained as doors rattling due to the howling gales. The same could also be said for the eerie whistling noises.

Despite several hours in the darkness of the Dockyard, the *Most Haunted* visit, like so many other paranormal investigations, could only produce the expected dramatics, providing an almost comedy element

The Joiners Shop.

The Most Haunted *team investigated the Joiners Shop in 2004.*

to proceedings. Strangely, despite the Dockyard being littered with very strong ghostly legends, the alleged spirits that Derek claimed to have sensed were previously unheard of, and no connection was made with the known ghosts.

Whatever your opinion is of paranormal activity, Chatham Dockyard remains one of the most likely places to experience something unusual. The ghost tours only scratch the surface of the dark history of the place and goodness knows what types of spirits lurk in those old buildings and dark corners. Are you brave enough to venture forth?

three

The Theatre Royal –

Things that go Hump(hrey) in the Night

I heard a noise. It was a faint noise, and, strain my ears as I might, I could not make out exactly what it was. It was a sound like a regular yet intermittent bump or rumble. Nothing else happened. There were no footsteps, no creaking floorboards, the air was absolutely still …

Susan Hill – *The Woman in Black*

The ornate façade of the Theatre Royal deceives the eye. The narrow front suggests that this once-glorious theatre only held a few, and yet more than 3,000 people would cram themselves into No.102 High Street to watch a variety of stars – from the likes of Sybil Thorndike, Ken Dodd, Harry Secombe, Charlie Chaplin and Norman Wisdom to comedy duo Morecambe and Wise. Owned by C. & L. Barnard and opened to the public in 1899 – it was formerly the Royal Hippodrome – the Theatre Royal now sits in a forlorn state over a century later. It closed in 1955. During its latter years, the theatre acted as a department store and warehouse. From the 1980s onward volunteers worked tirelessly to try to save this magical place,

The Theatre Royal, c. 1900s. (Image courtesy of Medway Archives)

but now its heart is empty. The *Kent On Sunday* of 26 January 2003 reported, 'Curtain finally falls on theatre campaign', after those hard-working campaigners finally threw in the towel on their beloved project. In 1992, the Theatre Royal Chatham Trust Ltd was formed, but a lack of funding – despite strong support from famous film stars, and even Her Majesty the Queen – meant that the weather-ravaged building, which had also succumbed to vandalism and age over the years, could no longer function as a business. Trust chairman Ken Tappenden commented in 2003, 'I would love to keep the façade of the building, as it was originally designed by architect George Bond.'

The theatre stands as an anachronism, a ghost amidst the hustle and bustle of the town, its windows mere empty eyes and its contents in such a state of dereliction that demolition seems the only choice. No longer can any visitor attempt to take a glimpse back into the past, because the balcony and stage, which stretched some 72ft in length, are unsafe to tread, and many a door leads to a yawning chasm. With new roads and businesses growing around its shell, the future for the Theatre Royal looks grim as scaffolding engulfs the ashen walls like some cruel, suffocating skeleton.

The Theatre Royal may succumb to demolition, but the memories remain. And so do the ghosts – although whether they still loiter outside of lore amongst the broken beams and dust-ridden panels no one knows.

The *Evening Post* of Friday, 30 September 1977, reported, 'Curtain up on memories', in relation to the theatre being taken over by Harwood's furniture store. A Chatham lady named Rose Stephenson, aged seventy-one, recalled fond memories of the theatre for the newspaper: 'I used to work in the performers' lodging house at the Paddock eight hours a day ... But Saturday night was always theatre night for me and my friend Dolly. We paid a shilling to get in and a bag of peanuts cost 2*d*.'

Theatre Roya,l c. 1990s. (Photograph by Joe Chester)

Rose also mentioned the Theatre Royal's most popular ghost story – that of Humphrey, a long-lasting spectre said to haunt the old building. She added: 'We were in the gallery and we went all cold, then as we looked into the box we saw this blue haze coming across. All of a sudden it disappeared and it felt warm again.'

According to the newspaper:

Rose Stephenson.

> Humphrey has not been seen since the store opened. Rose believes he moved across the road to the Empire Theatre, now also demolished. Where he is now no one knows but as Rose said: 'If he wants to come back to the theatre at least there will always be a bed for him.'

One of the most interesting things about some of Chatham's most haunted premises is the enduring nature of the ghost stories. In 1943 (as recorded by author W.H. Johnson), Alex Ludlow and Pat Willoughby, who were working at the theatre, had a spooky encounter with a spectral gentleman. They were rigging the lighting in the area known as the 'gods' when Mr Ludlow, glancing over his shoulder, observed a man standing by the staircase. Both men were suspicious of the character as it was very unusual for a stranger to be lurking about on the property.

'You shouldn't be here, mister!' warned Mr Willoughby, and with that the man walked straight through the closed doors. Both witnesses were unnerved to the extent that they fled the building. Three years later, an assistant stagehand from the Chatham Empire, accompanied by a stage electrician, had paid the theatre a visit in the hope of borrowing a spotlight or two. The witness, Jack Stolton, had keys to the theatre as it was closed at the time of his visit, and so he let himself in. The electrician had been held up with something, and so Jack made his way

into the silent theatre but noticed, upon turning on the lights, that there was someone looking down at him from the dress circle. Naturally, Mr Stolton thought it was the electrician and shouted for him to come down. Of course, when Mr Stolton reached the foyer he expected to see the electrician coming down the stairs but, instead, the electrician came in the entrance door, apologising for his lateness.

According to legend, and W.H. Johnson, 'It is said that Humphrey was a trapeze artist who made a serious error in performance in front of Edward VII. Deeply hurt, humiliated in fact by his failure, he is said to have hanged himself from the dress circle.'

Although there appears to be no proof of this suicide, there's no doubt that a male figure haunts the theatre. The *Chatham Observer* of 17 February 1957 ran an article by local ghost hunter Frederick Sanders under the heading, 'The ghost of the Theatre Royal', with Sanders reporting:

> Towards the end of 1954 I spent, from time to time, over a period of two months, a great deal of time trying to uncover the weird happenings at the Royal, and to find out if Humphrey really did exist. Perhaps it was Humphrey, an unseen presence, that I encountered that last night

The Theatre Royal encased by scaffolding, c. 2011.

I spent locked in the old theatre alone. In the early hours of a moonlit frosty morning, high up in a haunted dress circle something seemed to be about. With the hair on my head prickling, with the sense of the super-normal atmosphere about me, I stood, torch in hand, with but its silvery sliver of light between me and what?

On 25 February 1966 Humphrey was back in the *Chatham Observer*, under the heading, 'Theatre ghost can still be seen':

Ghost talk is in the air again. The story of Humphrey the ghost who used to haunt the old Theatre Royal, Chatham, was first told exclusively in the *Observer* some years ago. Now this interesting topic has been given new interest by the 'Ghost Story' of Mrs Joan Gibbs, of Rochester as revealed in the BBC's news programme last week.

Mrs Gibbs is really Mrs Joan Copley, a well-known actress at the Medway Little Theatre, who lives in Orion Road, Rochester. Mrs Copley told a reporter of the time when she saw Humphrey sitting watching a dress rehearsal at the Theatre Royal in the early 1950s when Grant Anderson was actor-manager there.

She described him as 'a happy ghost – not at all frightening', and added, 'At first I didn't realise he was a ghost, because he was so kindly looking, but then I felt a chill. The ghost stayed there some time and then moved along the back of the gallery, and was gone. When he was alive the real Humphrey used to go over the takings between Barnard's Theatre and the Theatre Royal where he was employed, and he was always terribly interested in the theatre.'

Mrs Copley's contention is that Humphrey can still be seen on the same theatre premises, which are now occupied as business premises by Halford's. She said she believed he only appeared at night when there was no noise and that he could still be seen in a store room, where the stage used to be. But the manager of Halford's, Mr E.A. Robinson, said that not one of his staff had, to his knowledge, seen the ghost, although everyone had heard of it.

The newspaper also went on to mention that ghostly music had been reported coming from the building, just after it became a shop. According to Frederick Sanders, an assistant at Harwood's had seen the 'Green Ghost', being 'the shining figure of a man who used to haunt a certain box in the theatre'.

Sylvia Flaherty, former Tiller girl and one of the 'principal initiators of the moves to save the Theatre Royal', allegedly had several encounters with Humphrey, describing the ghost as the guardian of the theatre, with the dress circle being his favourite haunt. According to Sylvia, 'He would sit in one of the front rows and watch a show and if he didn't like it he would get up and walk out.'

Humphrey has also been blamed for banging doors and numerous other inexplicable events. Although, there is also a rumour that a woman, in a long gown, also haunts the theatre. It could be argued that such an arena of entertainment has soaked up so much energy over the years that maybe, on occasion, these events are replayed; although the poltergeist activity suggests that the ghosts are very much in tune with the modern climate. A Trust

The rear of the Theatre Royal in 2011.

Director, named Roy Phillips, reported that hats and masks used one evening for a performance were put away in a cupboard, but the next day when he visited the theatre they were scattered about the place. On another occasion, when Roy was sweeping up, he, despite being sceptical of the ghost stories, became extremely unnerved and asked, 'If there is a spirit here, give me a sign,' and with that something crashed to the floor just 30ft away; but on inspection he found nothing. Seconds later there was another loud crash, even closer to Roy, which startled him greatly, but once again his search for some broken item or dislodged tile proved fruitless. On another occasion, when promoting *The Phantom of the Opera*, Roy put on a cassette of the music, which echoed throughout the theatre, but when he walked away from the tape player the music turned off. As Roy walked back to see what was wrong the music started up again.

Rather aptly, on Friday, 13 October 1995, the local *Adscene* reported 'Club aims for spook scoop', stating that:

> Humphrey, the resident spook at Chatham's Theatre Royal, has attracted interest from serious ghost hunters. The Ghost Club, formed more than 130 years ago – and whose members have included Charles Dickens and Sir Arthur Conan Doyle – approached the theatre's Trust Director, Colin Bourner, asking for permission to investigate Humphrey.

According to the newspaper, investigations officer Ruth Jarvis, who was born and bred in Chatham, was interested in carrying out an all-night vigil and investigation, using high-tech equipment.

The theatre had come to public attention after the newspaper had mentioned the experiences of Roy Phillips, and another Trust Director, John Vigar, who also came forward to report that he'd seen 'something' whilst visiting the theatre with Mr Bourner. Mr Vigar commented:

> I didn't know any of the history and hadn't looked anything up about it at all. As soon as I got in there and stood in the auditorium, I could see the boxes with red curtains behind them. I could actually see them and the people in them. The boxes were crowded with people looking out towards the stage area.

Mr Vigar glanced away from the boxes for a second and when he looked back the crowd were still present, but then in the blink of an eye everyone vanished. Mr Vigar added, 'I thought my eyes were playing tricks on me and I didn't like to say anything to Colin because he wanted me to get involved as a historian.'

Bizarrely, not long after his experience, Mr Vigar was shown a photograph of what the boxes used to look like, and he confirmed that that was exactly what he had seen.

Theatre Royal Conservationist Mary Swift reported her experience to *Adscene*. The newspaper stated, 'She and researcher Clive Thompson had forced open the doors of the dress circle one night and were sitting alone in the theatre, savouring the atmosphere, when the door – secured with a heavy iron hook in the wall – suddenly slammed shut.'

Mary said, 'This was followed by several footsteps distinctly coming towards us. We didn't speak or move – and under normal circumstances we should have been terrified. But we were aware of a strange, comforting presence – convinced that Humphrey had made his way to his favourite seat.'

Do the spirits of the past still peer from the original windows of the Theatre Royal?

nessed, or felt, for some thirty-five years, and the idea that the old building still houses six phantoms, is beginning, presumably like the ghosts themselves, to fade.'

The biggest issue with this haunting, as is the case with many ghostly tales, is not the inconsistency of the phantoms, but the inaccurate storytelling of some of the authors. For instance, in his *Ghost Hunter Walks in Kent*, Rupert Matthews, in reference to the ghost of Humphrey, states:

Richard Parker, a former chairman of the Friends of the Theatre Royal, reported that he'd smelled 'sweet tobacco smoke' in the theatre, despite the fact that smoking was banned in the theatre in the 1960s. However, this smell was also confirmed by another woman, who told Mr Parker that one afternoon she'd walked along a passage when she felt a sudden tap on her shoulder and a voice asked, 'Where's the major?'

In 1997 the *Kent Today* of 23 September reported 'Audience for a ghost' after a group of brave Girl Guides and Brownies assembled in the theatre to raise money, and in the hope of catching a glimpse of a ghost. Although no spirits were forthcoming, the girls raised £110 for the theatre.

Author Andrew Green recorded that: 'A certain amount of poltergeist activity was experienced by a group of policemen who went into the room where the disturbances had been reported. They noted the chaos of upturned chairs and tables, heard a couple of doors slamming and weird footsteps.' The policemen were so spooked they decided not to hang around to investigate the noises. Another police team were drafted in and experienced the same activity. However, Mr Green, in his book *Haunted Kent Today*, seems slightly sceptical of the Theatre Royal spirits, stating, 'No apparitions have actually been wit-

It is thought that he was an assistant manager who worked there in the 1920s and who, one day, failed to turn up for work. He seems to have cleared his rented room and left Chatham in a great hurry, only for his spectre to return a few weeks later.

Sadly, Matthews cites no sources for this information, or for the other ghost stories he mentions regarding the theatre. The author also mentions the ghost of the Green Man, a figure said to haunt one of the boxes which overlooks the stage. He remarks that: 'This phantom is dressed all in green: green suit, green tie, green shirt and presumably, if they could be seen, green shoes.' According to Matthews there is also the spirit of an old lady who has allegedly been seen on the ground floor, and furthermore he claims that the ghost of a young girl has been spotted near the toilets. According to Matthews:

The girl delights in unwinding the rolls of toilet paper, throwing the soap on the floor and such other annoying little habits. A policeman was in the shop one day in the early 1990s when a loud crash sounded from the wash room. The man raced in to find the cubicle door slamming to and fro without any human hands moving it.

Finally, Matthews goes on to mention the ghost of a chap named Charlie Monks, who was a 'former member of the front of house staff'.

Of course, the strength of many a good ghost story is its ability to be passed down through generations; over time, these tales are exaggerated, with details being added or subtracted, depending on the storyteller. Sadly, many seemingly genuine ghost stories are also ruined in this way, and, many years down the line, they bear little resemblance to their original structure.

Some of these tales may have been cited from Richard Parker, who when speaking about the theatre stated, 'Humphrey is our main ghost … [he] is the ghost who you can feel but can't see, the Green Ghost is the ghost you can see but can't hear, and Charlie's the ghost you can hear but can't see.'

The toilet ghost could well be one of two: either that of a woman who died in 1911, or, in the case of the younger girl, someone who lived nearby and died in an institution at the turn of the 1900s. There are also two previously unpublished stories which concern the father of Joe Chester. Joe's father was employed at the theatre in the 1930s as an odd-job man and scene-shifter. The first incident, although vague, took place when Joe's father was pulling a rope and something invisible brushed his side. On another occasion, whilst bending down backstage, he was confronted by an ethereal slim-looking figure attired in colourful costume.

One final attempt to solve the mystery of Humphrey comes from the *Chatham News* of 18 March 1974, in which it is written:

> The secret of the ghost at Chatham's Theatre Royal may have been solved by a man who started work at the theatre in 1917. Mr Charles Taylor of Castle Road, Chatham, said this week that the name of the mystery ghost was Frisby Bracknol. Mr Bracknol was an actor appearing at the theatre in a production called *Diana of Dobsons* in 1907 but he was thrown out for being 'permanently under the influence of alcohol'. The next week he was found hanged in one of the theatre's circle boxes. This version of the mystery ghost was told to Mr Taylor by an electrician when he started work at the theatre.

So, there you have it, the Theatre Royal of Chatham, a once ghost-infested arena which buzzed with light entertainment, but is now standing as a mere shadow of its former self. Do Humphrey and his fellow phantoms still loiter there, or have they departed the theatre along with the furnishings, leaving only dust and cobwebs?

Richard Parker.

four

Haunted Houses and Pubs

I could not sit still in that claustrophobic and yet oddly hollow-feeling old house …

Susan Hill – *The Woman in Black*

Ghost terror!

Everybody loves the idea of a haunted house: creaking floorboards, slamming doors, a flickering light bulb, a cold passageway and a dripping tap. However, not all reputedly haunted houses are old, and some stories are far removed from the almost pleasant spookiness created in fiction. The *Chatham Standard* of Tuesday, 14 August 1990, ran a

Fort Pitt Street once harboured a haunted house.

terrifying story on its front page under the bold heading: 'Mum's Ghost Terror', with Richard McComb reporting that a 'Priest [was] called to drive away evil spirits'.

According to the reporter:

Sinister spirits that have terrorised a Medway mother since childhood have been driven from her home in a special ceremony conducted by a priest. It is the fourth time the Revd Gilbert Spencer has tackled poltergeists within a quarter mile of Rachel Jolley's flat in Fort Pitt Street, Chatham. Rachel (22) says she has been terrified at night by the cries of a baby, noises in her bathroom and a deep voice whispering 'help me'.

A favourite picture of her two-year-old son Rikki has been thrown to the floor repeatedly. Mr Spencer, rector of St John's Church in Railway Street, told the *Chatham Standard*: 'A poltergeist is symptomatic of a presence of something nasty. I am convinced there is something in it. It is an area people shouldn't mess about with.'

Rachel has been driven to hysterics by the night time happenings. She said:

'You sometimes feel that something has walked through you, just momentarily. It's like death.'

Mr Spencer blessed each room of Rachel's flat and asked her to join in prayer.

'It is really to say, in God's name, whatever is evil, get out!' said Mr Spencer.

He said the poltergeists he had encountered in Chatham, always attached themselves to young women such as Rachel. And the young mum is no stranger to evil goings-on. She said a violent ghost brought terror to the lives of her family in Speedwell Avenue, Weedswood. It banged a wardrobe door and eventually shattered its glass. The furniture then became shrouded in a glow.

All the family were present when a priest and medium exorcised the spirit – all except Rachel, then aged thirteen, who believes she has been pursued ever since.

When paranormal activity reaches severe heights, priests are often called in to exorcise a property. (Illustration by Simon Wyatt)

'It's like it is following me,' she said.

Mr Spencer said poltergeists were quite common in Chatham. Police once called him to a home where a cupboard door had been wrenched from its hinges, and an electric fire thrown across the room.

'There is a kind of unseen energy,' said Mr Spencer. 'These are some of the things we cannot explain.'

Mr Spencer said someone came to him claiming to be possessed by the Devil, but the priest said he was not allowed to exorcise souls. And he warned of the dangers that could be unleashed by occult practices.

'Black magic and Ouija boards open up to a force of evil,' he said.

The unpleasant at Mount Pleasant

The *Chatham, Rochester & Gillingham News* of 15 August 1975 also ran a tale of a haunted house. The headline read: 'Rooms sprinkled with holy water – Priests called to house of mystery.' Barry Whelan reported:

Roman Catholic priests have visited a house in Chatham after reports that it may be haunted. A young Chatham mother, twenty-four-year-old Mrs Delena Whitehead lives at the house in Mount Pleasant with her four children.

'I don't believe in ghosts but after what has been happening here in the last few weeks I am getting a bit nervous,' she said.

Priests were called to the house by her friends after a series of mysterious incidents. The house has been blessed and rooms have been sprinkled with Holy Water. The series of so far inexplicable incidents started three weeks ago when Mrs Whitehead, who is separated from her husband, went downstairs at night to find

Mount Pleasant off Chatham Hill.

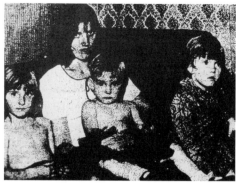

The Whitehead family. (Image courtesy of the Chatham, Rochester & Gillingham News)

her cat in a wild state in the living room, and her dog growling and trying to get out of the door. In the morning she found a hole in the back of her settee and a piece ripped from the front. The second incident happened a few nights later when Mrs Whitehead was again woken at night. She again went downstairs to her living room to find her furniture piled up in the middle of the floor. Events came to a head last week and over the weekend.

Mrs Whitehead said, 'On Monday or Tuesday morning last week I found cupboards open, cups all over the floor, chairs in the dining room all over the place and the television was flat out across the floor. I went to go out the front door to call a friend but I just couldn't. I know it sounds funny but there was something stopping me getting out. The place was quiet for three days. On Friday night I was told there was a big storm during the night. Every time it rains the house gets wet because I have a hole in the roof and a few weeks ago I was flooded out during a storm. The next morning a chap along the road was bailing out his cellar and asked me if I was badly flooded. I then realised that the house was as dry as a bone. Outside the yard was dry and a bucket in the yard didn't have a drop in it.

The same day I went shopping with my friend. We were standing on the steps outside my house when I felt a push from behind. I put my hand out to stop myself falling and at the same time she put her hand out. She just touched my head and a whole lot of my hair came out. We were the only two people on the step and there was nobody behind me. On Sunday morning about 2 a.m. my friend and I were sitting having a cup of tea when scratches suddenly began appearing on my face and on my chest. Other things have happened. An ornament and ashtrays have suddenly flown across the room into the wall and also the coffee table went across the floor. The place has become freezing cold all of a sudden and once when it was cold I began to get a burning pain in my back. When a friend took a look I had scratch marks all over my back. On Sunday cups just flew out of the cupboard. I have been renting this house for four years. It has always been peculiar but nothing like this.'

Mrs Whitehead also told the newspaper that two years previous she'd been grabbed by an invisible assailant in the vicinity of the back door. Police were called to find Mrs Whitehead standing outside with blood on her arm.

A Father John Hine, of St Michael's Church told the newspaper, 'I have witnessed nothing myself. I have had experience of similar cases and I know that it is incredible how things can escalate.'

He concluded, 'I have talked to Mrs Whitehead but there has been no talk of an exorcism. We will be keeping a watch on the situation.'

Joe's house of horror

I've often been of the opinion that some people are more susceptible to paranormal activity than others. I don't know why this is. Maybe it depends on the psyche of the individual. As I write this book I can honestly say that I've never seen a ghost, and yet some would deem that surprising considering I often spend dark and stormy nights in allegedly ghost-infested woods. One person who has been a big influence on my life is my mother's uncle, Joe Chester. He is one of those people who has, since childhood been surrounded by the supernatural. As a child Joe would give me creaky old books pertaining to ghosts and the unexplained, and I would be thrilled by some of his stories of visits abroad, and experiences with the paranormal.

Joe was born on the 17 September 1931 in a house at Rope Walk, a side turning of New Road, in Chatham. This house, no longer there, was extremely haunted. This is Joe's story.

I have no idea of how long the house had been in existence prior to my birth there; all I know is that we paid, if I recall correctly, 7s 6d (old money) per week to our landlord. The house had eleven so-called rooms in it: the three basement rooms had been referred to as cellars, for none of us actually lived in these. The first floor consisted of a kitchen, living room and front room, and above these were our sleeping quarters: one front room, one halfway along a short passage, and at the end a small room that we called a box room. This had been my bedroom.

I was to encounter my very first experience of the supernatural here in this little box room. Although I had been at that time a so-called tender, the uncanny experience had been real and not some nightmare suggested by my dear parents. I had been sent up to bed this evening with my little piece of candle stuck firmly in its holder. On the way upstairs I hummed to the music being broadcast on the wireless set from the living room, candle in one hand, and book under my arm. I had been told (by a strict father) that on no account must I begin reading this book whilst in bed.

Joe drifted off to sleep after a short while, but then he suddenly awoke. He was unsure of the time but he assumed it wasn't that late because he could still hear the wireless downstairs.

Feeling rather odd Joe decided, against his father's wishes, to thumb through his book of fairy tales whilst perched on the edge of his bed. After casting his eyes over the large words, Joe's attention was suddenly drawn to movement in the vicinity of the built-in cupboard. The door appeared to be slightly ajar. Joe's eyes went back to the book, and then once again back to the cupboard, and this time the door seemed further ajar. It was then that Joe felt a chill run up his spine.

'I had the feeling I was not alone in my little room,' he commented.

Joe looked to the right and there, sitting alongside him was, in his words, 'a shapeless white apparition'.

The figure, which was the size of an adult, had no face and what appeared to be hands were crossed in its lap. Despite its lack of distinguishing features, Joe felt that the spectre was staring at him, and after a few seconds young Joe, engulfed by fear, cast his book to the floor and fled the room, knocking the flickering candle to the floor.

Joe never slept in that box room again, but a month later Joe was heading off to bed, in another room, armed as always with his candle, and as he reached the summit of the stairs he saw, to his utmost horror, that same blurred 'face', whose lower legs seemed buried in the stairs. On this occasion Joe was not overcome by fear, and instead of descending the stairs he rushed straight towards the entity and ran straight through it and into his bedroom.

Joe's third encounter with that same wraith took place during daylight, quite a while after the stairway incident. One afternoon Joe was making his way up the stairs when to his astonishment he saw, coming round the bend at the top, a floating head! Joe fled back to the safety of the living room.

This was to be Joe's last encounter with the spectre at the Rope Walk house, although in 1975, whilst living in his current residence on the Weedswood Estate, he did see the ghoul again. One evening, Joe, his wife, and two daughters were finishing drinking tea in their living room, and Joe decided he'd take the cups to the kitchen to be washed up. Opening the kitchen door, Joe almost collided with that same frightful shade.

Going back to the New Road house, Joe, recalling those days, commented:

So many weird things had taken place within the walls of that old house; I find it a little difficult remembering, especially now that I am much older. One particu-

When Joe Chester was a child, residing at his home on the New Road, he was terrified by a floating head. (Illustration by Simon Wyatt)

lar frightening little incident is as follows: A day in particular, I believe it was a Sunday, whilst our parents were out, we [Joe and his brother Albert and sisters Rose and Doris] had grown tired of our pillow fight and a new game had been thought up. We called this harmless game 'On a night like this'. It went like this: one or two of us would be under the table, whilst a chosen one would go along the passage which led to our front door. My brother Albert had been chosen first. He would walk back to the living room door and knock on it loudly announcing, 'Are you coming out to play?', and we would answer in unison, 'What, on a night like this!' and then one of us would let the other in. Sometimes one of us would open the door after the other one had knocked, and refuse to go out on such a dreadful night. We each took turns at going along the passage. It had been Doris's turn next. All went well with her: knock, knock at the door, followed by the request to come out and play, up would get one of us from under the table, go to the door, open it and say, 'What, on a night like this!'– now comes the frightening bit.

It was now the turn of our elder sister Rose. Out went Rose along the passage. We listened to her steps as she came back to knock on the living room door. After her knock, knock, I got up and went to open the door. I opened it, and although she made the same request, and it was indeed her voice, I received a terrible shock, for superimposed over Rose's face … was another face: a ghostly image! I did my best to explain, and at that the game ended!

Quite a few weeks went by before Joe and his siblings played that game again, but when they did, the same thing happened. The superimposed face appeared once again over Rose, but this time it was Joe's brother Albert who saw the ghastly mask. On another occasion, whilst sitting in bed reading, Joe saw the ghost of a smiling man in a brown suit. Another time the house was visited by strange, blue lights which would zip about the place. On one occasion the family cat, Ol' Man, was frantically scratching at the living room door as Joe was sitting talking to his mother. Joe got up from his chair to let the cat out into the passage, but then the cat began scratching at the cellar door. Joe's mum motioned to let the cat down into the cellar, thinking that maybe Ol' Man had sensed a rat or heard a scurrying beetle. When Joe creaked open the cellar door the cat froze, then turned and scampered back to the living room. As Joe peered into the darkness he saw strange blue orbs

on the stairs – the same light phenomena he'd seen previously on the garret stairs. On another occasion, Doris – when aged about seven – had a spooky encounter with a strange, tall whitish 'thing' whilst she was shovelling coal in the cellar. Doris came screaming upstairs and told her mother that an apparition had emerged from the adjoining, cobweb-ridden cellar.

These frightening incidents were sewn together by various other, yet less terrifying, events: objects within the house moved of their own accord, strange noises were heard, the pet cat kept staring at something that no one else could see, and there were peculiar light phenomena. To some, just typical haunted house activity. However, this activity would seemingly follow Joe around and it would be fair to say that every house Joe has resided in has seen some degree of paranormal activity. Joe's life has been rife with strangeness, and not just activity that only he has witnessed. There is such a wealth of stories that they could fill their own volume. However, I have never once doubted Joe, or the experiences of his family.

One particular story, which always springs to mind, concerns my sister Vicki, who, as a child in the early 1990s, would often visit Joe at his Weedswood Estate residence with our mother. Vicki must have been about five years old at the time, and whilst now she fails to remember the incident, Joe and my mother recall it clearly. One afternoon my mother was chatting to Joe in the kitchen when my sister suddenly pointed to a dog that she could see. Vicki was quite frightened by the spectral animal, especially because neither my mother nor Joe could see it. Although Joe had owned cats, and believes that one or two may still haunt the house, he has never owned a dog.

Magpie Hall Road

Peter Underwood is considered one of the finest authors in regards to collecting stories of the supernatural. In his book, *A Gazetteer of British Ghosts,* he records a Chatham spectre, stating:

> Two neighbouring houses in Magpie Hall Road are reported to have been haunted at night for over twenty years by unexplained noises, rappings and footsteps – noises which always stopped when a light was switched on. Time after time, the occupants told me, footsteps, followed by rapping as though someone wanted to come in, were heard from the vicinity of the stairs and bedrooms; sometimes the rapping sounded louder and more violent than at others but always it stopped when a light was switched on. It usually began about midnight and sometimes went on till about 5 a.m. Years ago a man committed suicide in one of the houses by cutting his throat and in the same house a previous occupant complained that she had seen a 'form' she could not account for.

Sadly, Mr Underwood fails to give the exact location of the house – rather frustrating considering that the road is so long; another author, Antony D. Hippisley Coxe also mentions the Magpie Hall Road

haunting, albeit briefly. However, Peter Underwood, in his book *Ghosts of Kent*, seems rather sceptical of the ghost story, adding, '… a psychical researcher friend, who lives in Chatham, tells me he has no convincing evidence.'

There is another ghost story from Magpie Hall Road, which comes from the files of Joe Chester. According to Joe:

> Another strange case pertains to a chap I worked with in Chatham Dockyard, and who had lived at that time in a house at the bottom of Magpie Hall Road. He was really in a state whenever he arrived at work. He had a lot of trouble with his wife, who was apparently seeing another man at the time. Not only did he go on and on about this affair regarding his wife and her lover, but [he] actually had to go on occasions to be locked up in a Canterbury prison, for refusing to pay her maintenance. My friend was in so much bother that, on top of all this, he had to put up with his house being haunted. The local vicar had been called to his house on one occasion, to try and exorcise this troublesome entity but it proved fruitless. The vicar tried to be friendly with the ghost by reaching out his hand to the unseen entity, only to have his arm pulled into the 'unknown'… But the vicar, on seeing a loaf of bread rise from off the table, vacated the house more quickly than he had gone in!

According to Joe, the weirdest episode of this haunting took place when his friend was in prison. He said that whilst in his cell he'd been visited by the same apparition that was haunting his house. The witness claimed that he'd observed the ghost at his Magpie Hall Road residence, and spoke to it, and that the spirit even told the man the name of his wife's lover!

Nan and Granddad's house and others

My wonderful grandparents Ron and Win lived at Sturla Road in Chatham. This steep hill sits in the shadow of the Great Lines. As a child, I would often stay at my nan and granddad's house; for me it was always a magical place, even though a few of the family were always slightly spooked by the back bedroom. We used to call it the 'blue room', but this was mainly down to the décor, although, it was often rather cold in there when the rest of the house was warm. Despite the odd atmosphere of the 'blue room', it was my grandparents' bedroom which seemed to be haunted.

My grandparents used to own two cats, and after the cats had died my granddad recalled how one night, whilst getting into bed, he felt one of the animals brush against his leg. On another occasion, during the late '80s, my nan entered the bedroom to do a bit of a spring clean. She noticed that the chair in the room had been moved from its original position by the wall to the middle of the room. She thought nothing of it, and blamed my granddad, although he denied moving the chair. However, soon afterwards the same thing happened, and she also found that some ornaments had been turned around. After this strange episode, no further spectral redecorating took place. On another occasion my grandparents took their daughter Susie to the Isle of Wight for a holiday. My dad was keeping an eye on the house in their absence. One day he dropped in to check everything was okay, only to hear voices coming from the bedroom upstairs. Thinking there was an intruder, my dad ran upstairs to investigate, only to be met by deafening silence.

My grandparents became good friends with their neighbours, a lovely lady named Iris Cooper, and her husband Bill. In the 1940s, Iris and Bill sadly lost their son Robert; but one night, during the '60s, Iris awoke and saw a little boy kneeling at the foot of their bed. His elbows were resting on the mattress and he cupped his chin in his hands. The figure gradually faded into nothing, but Iris was to see this apparition on three more occasions.

My mother's mum, Doris, died in 1966 at a young age, leaving behind her husband Ted (my other granddad) and four daughters. Shortly after her death, my mum was making her bed when she saw, albeit fleetingly, her mum, Doris. She was wearing a red dress. My mother's uncle, Ken, also claimed to have seen Doris (his sister) whilst he was at his home in Yarrow Road, on the Weedswood Estate. She appeared in her death vestments – a pink gown with a golden cross on the chest. Her ghost actually made contact with him: she brushed his throat. Bizarrely, a few days later Ken was struck down with a bad throat.

Another ghost story concerns family on my father's side. My dad's uncle, Bill, who often told me ghost stories as a child, mentioned that when his son Tony was born, a friend staying at the house reported seeing the figure of a man standing over the cot. The person who saw the figure said that the 'ghost' was wearing a cap and a scarf and was on crutches – this figure would have been my great-grandfather, William George, who was known as 'Sticks', as the Second World War had claimed one of his legs.

Another story concerning Bill took place at his house on the White Road Estate. One night, during the early 1970s, after Bill and his wife Pat had put their children to bed, something odd happened. The children's bedroom door was extremely stiff and difficult, if not impossible for the children to open, but they managed to get into Bill and

Pat's bedroom, waking them up. Bill, with a start, asked, 'How did you lot get out?'

To which they replied, 'The old man let us out!'

This happened on a couple of occasions until Bill decided to call in an exorcist. The family all kneeled and prayed whilst the priest sprinkled holy water around the house. Every door was left open and, all of a sudden, cold air seemed to flush through the building. After that the supernatural occurrences ceased.

Later investigations revealed that the previous owner's father had died in the room where the kids had been sleeping.

Not all creaking houses are haunted however. One story which still makes me chuckle concerns Bill's brother Buster, who, during the '80s resided at a house on the Weedswood Estate. Strangely, something seemingly paranormal took place, the family would always call on my granddad, Ron, to deal with it. On this occasion Buster reported that the house was being plagued by banging noises. My granddad visited the house and after a quick inspection found the cause of the 'haunting' to be nothing more than vibrating pipes.

I have so many stories passed down from my family concerns ghosts that they probably merit a book of their own, but one last haunted house story I must mention concerned an old friend of mine named Brett. Brett used to be my neighbour when I lived on the Weedswood Estate, and he would tell me about a strange, supernatural eye that often appeared on his bedroom wall at night. This eye manifested on many occasions and Brett was so terrified that he would run from the room and often meet his mother coming the other way. The eye would materialise on the headboard of his bed then move around the walls, and even if Brett was brave enough to approach it, he could never get close to it.

Another childhood friend of mine, named Russell, told me in 2011 that his mother, whilst living in a house on Yarrow Road, did, on one occasion, have a meeting with a ghostly woodsman! This strange encounter took place a few decades ago.

Incident at Prospect Row

During the 1950s, with the Second World War a fading memory, many derelict houses stood in Chatham, which were set to be demolished. However, my granddad Ron, accompanied by a friend, decided they could make a bit of a killing by going into these old properties and stealing some of the fireplaces. One particular house, at Prospect Row, had been emptied of its furniture but its impressive fireplace still stood. One afternoon my granddad peered through the dusty window and eyed the fireplace, deciding that he would return to retrieve it. When my granddad came back the following night, at about 8 p.m., he intended to get into the house and chisel out the fireplace. The fact that it was pitch-black made the task rather difficult and it was such a warm, still night that they had to be careful not to make too much noise – easier said than done when one is attempting to steal

Prospect Row.

an entire fireplace from the wall. My grand-dad and his mate came in via the front door, which led straight to the living room. As it was rather humid, they left the front door open, but I'm also guessing that doing this made it easier for them to get the fireplace straight out.

My granddad began chipping away at the old fireplace when his mate noticed that the door, despite there not being a breath of wind, had begun to swing to and fro on its hinges. Four times it did this before suddenly slamming shut with an almighty bang. Immediately, both men assumed someone was outside mucking about, because neither man had any time for ghosts. When they looked outside there was no one about and so my grand-dad continued chiselling out the fireplace. However, when the door began to swing again, of its own accord, my granddad's mate decided something strange was afoot and wanted to get the fireplace out before anything stranger happened. They removed the fireplace, but my granddad's friend refused to return to the area.

Although my granddad and his family experienced many strange things, I'm not sure if he was a great believer in the super-natural. But whenever he was talking about ghosts he would tell me, 'They can't hurt you, but if you ever come face to face with one, always ask it what it wants.' On that dark, humid night at Prospect Row in the 1950s, asking a ghost what it wanted was the last thing on my granddad's friend's mind!

The lady at a Luton house

In late 2009, my sister Vicki lived in a house just off Luton High Street, Chatham. Around Christmas time my sister began receiving Christmas cards addressed to a woman named Margaret, who Vicki assumed used to live at the property. She was correct … and the woman had also died there. One night, Vicki was standing in the room leading to the front door when a misty figure emerged from the region of the fireplace and rushed towards her. Vicki didn't have time to move, and the appari-tion, which she said appeared briefly in a whitish cloth dress, glided straight through her. Vicki gasped as the entity seemed to pass through her.

The house on Lordswood Lane

Lordswood, which is situated not far from Walderslade, has a ghost story which I found tucked away in a document writ-ten by a member of the Medway Archives & Local Studies Centre. Under a heading of 'Mysterious Medway or: A Ghost Story for Christmas', the author, only identifying herself as 'Charon', wrote:

The owner of a fairly new house in Lordswood Lane came in to enquire about the history of the area with par-ticular reference to previous owners of the land. During the course of our inves-tigation, the enquirer, an intelligent and seemingly rational being, became increas-ingly anxious. He eventually related that he had become so depressed that he was not able to work and was receiving treat-ment from his doctor. The cause of his depression was his house, or rather the unseen occupant who watched his every move, a presence filled with resentment and hatred. His wife was totally unaware of this entity and was extremely happy in their home, resisting all attempts to be persuaded to sell up and move. The enquirer had reached the end of his tether, teetering between divorce and suicide. However, new neighbours had moved in next door and within days of their arrival, the new occupant called around and introduced himself. After passing the usual pleasantries, the new neighbour announced that he too hated his house and hoped to move again as soon as he could persuade his wife to do so. He felt idiotic to say so, but had the feeling that something evil was watching him day and night: his wife felt nothing of the kind. After listening to the enquirer's story, they agreed that a previous male owner of the land must be jealously guarding the property, however it was not possible to prove who this owner was. In the end, and as a last resort, the current owners approached the Church and had their properties blessed.

Strangely, the wooded area close to the houses is known as Cats Brain Wood – a mysterious name if ever there was one. It surely is just a coincidence, but since the early 1980s there have been sightings around Lordswood of a huge black cat, resembling a black leopard or panther. I saw this animal twice in 2000 and another individual in 2008. With a lifespan of approximately thirteen years, the animal that has been seen around the area in the present day is clearly not the same individual reported decades ago – a breeding population, perhaps?

Princes Park poltergeist

In 2000 a woman working at Luton library was approached by two women who had an unusual query. They enquired about the houses they were living in – as neighbours – at Princes Park. According to the two women, they had only lived at their properties for a short time but both had experienced severe bouts of paranormal activity, to the extent that each had contacted the council and asked to be moved somewhere else.

So unsettled were they by the strange goings-on in their homes that they wanted to find out the history, so they could try to solve the mystery. In 2011 I spoke to the woman who had lookd into the query. She said:

> The houses, within the vicinity of Street End Road, may well have had connections to a death at an old glue factory which at the time I knew nothing about. However, quite a while later, I found out that a glue factory of sorts was situated in the region of Epps Farm around 100 years ago. It seems that someone died during a tragic accident and that the neighbourhood, many years later, suffered increasing bouts of ghostly activity. The two women were terrified and told me they'd asked for help from a spiritualist, and a séance was conducted and the information about the factory death came about.

Although I was not able to find out the exact location of the haunting, legend has it that no one has stayed for long in the houses due to the poltergeist activity.

Cross Street chills

During the 1960s, some of the houses at Cross Street in Chatham sat in a state of dereliction and were due to be demolished. A woman named Judy, who was a child at the time, recalled how she and some friends had decided to give one of the old houses a visit one afternoon; they entered via the rear access to avoid detection. Being kids they were curious about the creepy house and were brave enough to descend the dusty steps into the cellar which ran to the front of the house and underneath the front room. Whilst in the dank basement they all suddenly heard the front door open and the sound of heavy footsteps travel across the floor. The terrified kids thought they'd been rumbled and that a police officer was present. The children waited with bated breath in the gloom of the cellar, but the footsteps suddenly ceased. After a few minutes of suspense, the children decided to make their way upstairs and to flee out the front door. To their shock, when they reached the front door – the same door by which the 'person' had entered – they found that it was nailed up and that there was no way in or out via it. The children believed they'd heard a ghost and scampered out the way they'd first entered, not once passing another human.

Judy recalled how she had spoken to her father about the house, but he warned her not to stray there again. According to Judy, when her father was a child he used to run errands in the area and on one occasion heard the woman in that particular house calling. Apparently, her calls were in terror because seconds later she was murdered by her husband with an axe!

High Street horror

During late October 2011, I was contacted by a lady named Lisa Birch who mentioned a poltergeist story from No. 222 High Street, Chatham. She emailed the following:

Nellie and Charlie Piper, along with their son David and daughter Margaret, lived in the property. The building was three storeys high, and at the top it used to be a Hairnet Factory. It had no lights at all in this part of the building.

This tale originates from the mid-1940s, just after the War. My mum, Margaret Piper, was about seven or eight years old at the time. She slept in a huge bedroom with her parents. She cannot remember where her brother was at the time.

One night, not long after going to bed, a large picture which was on the bedroom wall suddenly lifted off the wall and crashed to the floor breaking the glass (it definitely did not fall off the wall). Then the door into a very dark small passageway, leading to the lounge over the shop, opened and slammed shut. As you can imagine my grandparents and mum were terrified! My grandparents investigated to see if they could see anything that would have caused this to happen, but with no luck. They then also found that a white statue of a lady, which was in the lounge on a table, had been beheaded! Her head was lying at her feet.

My mum remembers that the passageway outside the bedroom always had a peculiar feeling. My mum and gran hated it and always ran through it at top speed. Many years later mum found out that her cousin also hated the passageway, but he had never mentioned it before. The day after the spooky event, my grandfather opened a damper in the fireplace, just above from where the picture came off the wall, and discovered a lot of human hair.

Chatham High Street. (Image courtesy of Medway Archives)

Along with houses, pubs always seem among the most likely places to harbour a ghost. Is this down to the fact that many public houses have stood for centuries and have residual energy? Or, as some sceptics might ask, is the resident 'ghost' merely the product of too many late-night drinking sessions?

An unseen presence

The *Chatham Standard* of 8 November 1988 reported, 'Strange spirit found in pub', stating that: 'A series of ghostly goings-on in a Chatham pub has led the landlord to think that he lives with a poltergeist.' According to the newspaper, landlord Ron Field, 'who runs the Good Intent in New Road, with his wife Lou', had reported on many occasions that doors had opened of their own accord and that any pets that had resided in the pub had been petrified by the alleged presence.

Mr Field told the newspaper:

When we first came to the pub in May we had a cat, which was very docile and never ran away from our old home. But as soon as we moved in it seemed terrified. The cat

darted outside and up a tree. After about a week it ran away and never came back.

Mr Field also mentioned that the doors of the fire escape had on occasion been seen to open by themselves and that a customer, who often brought his pet dog with him, remarked on there being a strange atmosphere – which was confirmed when his dog bolted upstairs and hid in the lavatory! Ron once said that, 'Two weeks ago a picture fell off the wall in the pool area. Everyone shouted out that they did not knock it off. The nail was still in the wall when the picture was on the ground.'

The pub, at No.50, closed down during the 1990s. It is now an Indian restaurant.

A chill at Churchill's

Churchill's – now known as the Brook Bar – is a public house which sits at No.7, The Brook, within the shadow of the Town Hall. In 2006, the pub had a newsworthy ghost. The *Medway Messenger* of 4 August 2006 reported 'Pub's broken clock is now tickety-boo', after a set of mysterious happenings. The newspaper reported:

Time has stood still at Churchill's for more than twenty years. In all that time the clock in the main bar of the Chatham pub has never been known to move except once when it started going backwards. But now, the 100-year-old clock is not only running, but keeping good time.

'I can't understand it,' said manager Michael Fernandez. 'It's an electric clock but very old. It was installed when the pub – which used to be the Army and Navy – was built, round about the same time as the Chatham Town Hall. During the nine years we've been here it's been stuck at quarter to seven. The previous tenants were here for twelve years and during that time they never knew it to work.'

And the mysteriously activated clock is not the only strange happening at Churchill's. Michael's brother, Alan, will not stay at the pub after a picture suddenly started swinging on its hanger through 180 degrees. When Michael was alone in the bar a voice clearly called out 'Can I have a pint please?'

Early one morning he saw his mobile phone move from the side table by his bed to a different location. And staff will not go into the cellar at midnight because of strange noises and a cold sensation.

'I've got used to it over the years,' said Michael, 'But some of the staff really don't like it.'

Hocus pocus at the Hare & Hounds

The Hare & Hounds used to sit on the Chatham/Rochester border. The *Chatham Standard* of 2 April 1975 mentioned that the then landlords, Frank and Sylvia Fallows, believed the pub to be haunted. Frank told the newspaper, 'I was down there (the cellar) one day and found that the gas had been turned off. I didn't do it and nobody else in the building had been down there. To this day I can't explain it. If there is a ghost down there it must be a friendly one because it makes sure my beer comes up all right.'

Intriguingly, the pub was said to have been built on an old graveyard and there were also rumours that a man had hanged himself in the cellar.

The Brook Bar, formerly Churchill's.

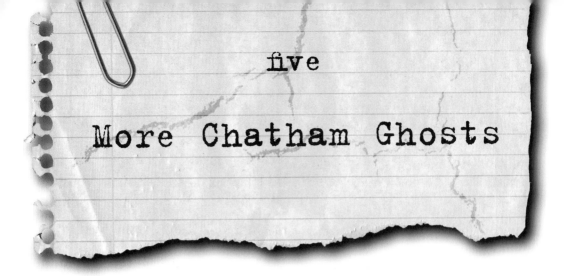

five

More Chatham Ghosts

The phantom sausage slasher!

Whether you believe in ghosts or not, there is no doubting that each year hundreds, if not thousands, of people claim to have a supernatural encounter. Whilst in some instances there appear to be sinister forces at work, other stories are of a quirky nature. For instance, the *Evening Post* of Friday, 10 January 1969, reported on the 'Sausage slashers at work', with a report saying that:

> The phantom sausage slashers – that mysterious band of men who specialise in banger bashing – have struck in Chatham High Street. Their target: Kemsley's butcher shop.
>
> When the shop closed yesterday the sausages were all tied together. But when manager Mr P.G. Gordon opened this morning, he could hardly believe his eyes. Vandals had cut through every single link.
>
> He commented later: 'Obviously the intruders were upset because there was nothing to steal, so they took their spite out on the sausages.'

No one was apprehended for the bizarre crime, leaving some to conclude that a ghost was at work!

The creep of Capstone Park

A few years back, a cousin of mine named Mark was camping, with friends, in the vicinity of Capstone Park – a nature reserve in Chatham. The park stretches for over 100 acres, and includes a small lake. On this particular night, the teenagers had retired to their tent, shying away from the chilly wind that was stirring the leaves in the park. During the early hours, Mark awoke and peered from the opening in his tent; he could see what he at first took to be a polythene bag in the distance, blowing in the wind. Mark slowly climbed out of the tent, but as he got closer to the object he realised that it was a figure that resembled an old man. The eerie apparition seemed to be rocking sideways on its two legs. Unnerved by the strange wraith, Mark crept back into his tent and hid himself in his sleeping bag as he waited for the cloak of night to fade into dawn.

The Bridgewood Manor Hotel phantom

Bridgewood Manor Hotel sits on the Bridgewood Roundabout, in Walderslade Woods. It is a 4-star hotel with over 100 rooms. A few years ago someone contributed a story to the BBC Weird Kent page. The person, who worked at the hotel, claimed:

> I was at work and doing my usual rounds at the hotel, and checking vacant rooms. I walked into one room and I heard a strange clicking noise. I searched the room, but of course, being a vacant room, no one could possibly be in there. I did what I had gone in the room to do, and then as I was leaving I saw something in the tall mirror out of the corner of my eye. The mirror reflects the bedroom, which I had just checked thoroughly, and in the mirror, I saw a woman in a white blouse, sitting on the bed. I looked into the room, to make sure I hadn't imagined it, and the woman was in fact there, pale faced, staring at me. I ran from the room, and checked the computer. The room was definitely vacant. The hotel has had several cases of ghost sightings, and this was mine. ...

On another occasion, a male witness woke in the middle of the night and to his horror saw a man standing near the foot of the bed staring at him. The man, wearing a pale, checked shirt, was around twenty-five or thirty years of age. The witness blinked his eyes to make sure he wasn't dreaming and then noticed that the figure was even closer. After a few seconds the apparition began to fade.

Interestingly, the woods around the hotel could hold the key to unlocking one of Kent's most intriguing and eeriest ghost stories –

The Bridgewood Manor Hotel.

that of the phantom woman said to haunt Blue Bell Hill. In 1916, a young woman was found murdered in what was then known as Bridge Woods. In the past – mainly since the 1960s – there have been sightings along the stretch of road, leading towards Blue Bell Hill and Maidstone, of a woman in a pale dress. Many believe the ghost is one of the victims of a terrible accident which took place in 1965, but this seems highly unlikely; especially as one of the first recorded encounters with a phantom hitchhiker took place in 1934. For more information read my book, *Haunted Maidstone*.

The sinister skull, from the, held by Enzo Cornacchia (left) and a friend. (Courtesy of the Evening Post*)*

Haunted hotel

'Was it a ghost that went bump in the night?' asked the *Evening Post* on 7 August 1968, following strange disturbances at 'the old hotel next to the Gibraltar Service Station, New Road Avenue, Chatham.' The newspaper reported that there had been rumours for many years that the building was haunted but, 'no-one ever dared tempt the spirits.' However, two men from Northfleet decided to conduct a ghost investigation in the old hotel, along with petrol station forecourt attendant Jenny Harkinson. She told the *Post*, 'Although I was petrified at the time I decided to join them on the ghost hunt. They laid paper crosses on the floor and then we went upstairs.'

According to Jenny, a loud bang came from downstairs and upon investigation the trio found the crosses strewn about the place. The men were of the opinion that the ghost would not appear, but later on that evening Jenny reported seeing, ' … what looked like a cloud of mist above the bathroom door. It was uncanny.'

The case of the sinister skull

Although not a ghost story, one of my favourite macabre tales in relation to Chatham could have its origins in the practice of black magic. Although the practice of 'witchcraft' has often been inaccurately portrayed in the media, some cases of alleged magic have hinted at dark dabbling. In many cases where diabolical summoning has reputedly taken place, animal skulls have been discovered, as if they have been used for sacrifice or morbid decoration. Alleged black magic rituals have also been held responsible for the appearance of supernatural entities.

During the 1970s, a stir was caused by a peculiarly morbid discovery in an old chimney at a house on Luton Road. The story made the local *Evening Post,* which reported: 'The sinister looking blackened skull, with two brass cups, came to light as Mr Cornacchia was fitting a new fireplace at his home … it must have been in the chimney for at least twenty years.'

The biggest mystery, however, was not the fact that such an oddment had been found, but what animal it had belonged to. The skull was quite large. The newspaper stated:

There is difference of opinion about the mystery skull. Mr Cornacchia's thirteen-year old son, Enzo, took it to school where a teacher identified it as belonging to a wild boar. But another expert at his sister's school thought it was a tiger. And at Rochester Museum they say firmly: 'It is a bear, you can tell by the teeth.'

So, dear readers, as this case is over thirty years old, and the photograph rather hazy, I hope you can solve the mystery as to what exactly had a skull this size. The newspaper concluded:

> Animal skulls are popular accessories among witchcraft devotees. Rams are most widely used, but there would appear to be nothing in the rules against bear skulls. Mr Cornacchia has no immediate plans for the skull. At the moment he is keeping it in the garden.
>
> 'It is not very pretty,' he said.

The road ghost

Britain is littered with haunted roads. No real surprise when you consider how many fatal accidents occur each year. Without a shadow of a doubt, Kent's most haunted stretch is Blue Bell Hill, which is a few miles short of Maidstone. The ghostly goings-on at this location have been mentioned in my book *Haunted Maidstone*. Another reputedly haunted road is Ash Tree Lane, situated at the back of what is known as Luton Wreck. During the 1970s, a woman was driving some friends home at 3 a.m. when suddenly, a woman with long greyish hair and wearing a long grey dress and bonnet appeared from nowhere. The vehicle nicked the woman but when the driver looked in the rear-view mirror there was no sign of her.

Doodlebug

Many years ago I worked at a telecommunications company situated near Rochester Airport. The building was said to be haunted by a former employee, but whilst there I spoke to a woman who claimed she was psychic. She mentioned to me that during the 1980s, whilst residing at her home in Chatham, she had a very weird encounter.

'I was with friends,' she said, 'and we were coming out of my house and [we] all looked up and saw a doodlebug.'

Doodlebugs, also known as a V-1 flying bomb, or buzz bomb, were developed during the Second World War by the German Air Force, so what on earth was one doing in the skies over England several decades later?

The witness believed she'd seen a phantom doodlebug, and although this sounds bizarre, in the past there have also been

The phantom doodlebug. (Illustration by Simon Wyatt)

numerous sightings across the world of phantom war planes. Are these military objects simply recordings of raids over Britain being replayed back to those susceptible enough to experience them?

The small phantom dog

In folklore there is mention of a ghastly spectre known as the hellhound, or Black Dog. These calf-sized, fiery-eyed monsters are often considered as a bad omen, and should you, on a dark and stormy night, be followed by such a frightful apparition then legend has it that someone in your family is about to die! The spectral canid my mother saw in the 1990s, however, was not a malevolent form. My mother had been suffering from pleurisy and was sitting up in bed at home. She was wide awake when she spotted something on her chest of drawers. She could clearly see that the form was a small, black dog with long floppy ears. My mum rubbed her eyes, and then once again stared

intently at the dog which gradually began to fade. A few days later my mother recovered from her illness and believed the small, ghostly dog had been a good omen.

...and the big phantom cat!

I've often wondered if, in the realm of the supernatural, phantom dogs chase ghostly cats! During the 1950s a very peculiar incident took place at the Victoria Gardens, a small open space which backs on to New Road, joining Chatham and Rochester. One evening, a man walking across the field in the area of the Victorian bandstand was startled to see a 'huge cat which resembled a lion'. The animal was prowling in the dusk and slinked away. Now, around this time, and especially into the swingin' '60s and early '70s, there began a spate of sightings across Britain pertaining to what were described as large, elusive 'big cats'. Whilst many of these reports were nothing more than misinterpretation, there was a core of

Victoria Gardens.

reports suggesting that people were in fact seeing animals such as puma, black leopard and a lynx. But a lion – surely not! With a lion being a social animal, such a creature would have stuck out like a sore thumb and been sighted regularly. So, if such a beast had escaped from somewhere then it would have been relatively easy for authorities to have recaptured it. The fact that no human fatalities occurred, and that no further reports were made, could suggest that the terrified witness had seen a spectral lion! Why it chose to haunt this spot we'll never know.

Eldon Street – once the haunt of phantom horses.

Only ghouls of horses!

One story, which I recall with a degree of haziness but some horror, concerns a ghostly horseman said to have haunted a patch of woods around Walderslade. I remember as a child being told this story by my relative, Joe Chester, who claimed that one of the local newspapers – he couldn't recall which – featured an amazing story claiming that the police had been called out to investigate a headless man mounted upon a ghostly horse. Joe believed the story had originated in the 1930s or '40s. The story goes that the horse and rider would thunder through the thickets and then disappear into a patch of mist that hid some water at the bottom of what is known as Waterworks Hill. Joe recalled that one evening, being keen to investigate the story, he and a few of his family members had ventured to the woods but were met by the Royal Engineers, who, according to Joe, had barricaded the road and fired at the spectre – their bullets passing through it. Rumour also has it that the phantom horseman was in fact 'caught' by the authorities. A very bizarre, albeit unlikely tale, but one which

may have been confused with a story mentioned in Michael Hervey's 1968 book, *They Walk By Night*, in which he speaks of a similar occurrence but elsewhere in Kent, at Canterbury. Hervey records that: 'Police had been alerted to watch out for a flying ghost horse', after a Miss Dorothy Ramsay, whilst driving late at night in the vicinity of Littlebourne Road, had seen the spectral horse which flew into the air and landed on top of her sports car.

In the black of night, Waterworks Hill is quite a creepy location. At the very bottom, mist tends to gather and the temperature drops. A few years ago, a couple driving home to their house at the White Road Estate were travelling down the hill when they noticed an old woman. It was during the early hours of the night so the woman wasn't waiting for a bus, and as the couple drove by they looked behind and noticed that she had vanished.

Another ghost horse story originates at Eldon Street. During the 1950s there was mention of a peculiar ghost said to haunt the area. The legend goes that a white horse, leading two smaller, brown horses, had been observed on the street. A woman named Judy – mentioned earlier in the book – claimed that her mother had heard of the story but one night was startled to hear horses' hooves clattering up the street. When she looked out of the window, she was stunned to see the trio of spectral horses. Some people believed that in life the horses belonged to a woman who resided at Cage Lane and that the animals used to disappear in that area. When the houses were eventually demolished there were no further sightings of the ghostly horses.

This legend, or one very similar, was confirmed when during the autumn of 2011, I received an email from a Derek Hargrave, who said:

> I was living along Luton Road and sometime between 1959 and 1960 I was wakened when I heard the loud clatter of horses trotting along Luton Road, I'd say around midnight. I turned over and went back to sleep. A couple of days later I read a very short item in the local papers stating that many residents had heard these horses but had not seen anything. The next time I heard these horses I got out of bed and leaned out of the window but could see only a deserted street, as you would expect at about midnight. The sound of the horses hooves was very loud and exaggerated by the sound reflecting off the walls of the terraced houses. The noise was directly below me and moving at a trotting pace towards Luton. It would be difficult to guess how many (invisible) horses there were because of the echo off the house walls, but I would say six - eight.

The spook of Snob!

Chatham High Street attracts thousands of people every week, so it's not surprising that there aren't many ghostly tales connected to it – spooks probably wouldn't be able to make themselves known amongst the hustle and bustle of eager shoppers. Mind you, ghost-hunter Andrew Green spoke of one particular wraith in his book, *Our Haunted Kingdom*, which haunted a shop called Snob Boutique, which used to sit at No.122 High Street. This shop, which sold clothes for women, and other garments, had a bout of paranormal activity during the late 1960s and early '70s. It began one day when one of the shop assistants spotted a female 'customer' on the security video standing by a rail of dresses combing her hair. However, the woman seemed to be dressed in old-fashioned clothes. Intrigued by the shopper, the member of staff left the security room and went on to the shop floor, only to find no sign of the woman. However, when she went back to the 'viewing room' she could still see the female figure on the screen, brushing her locks. According to Green, the assistant called over five members of staff who 'returned upstairs and were astonished to find the potential customer was nowhere to be seen. The television system was checked and found to be in perfect order'.

Shortly after this peculiar occurrence, there was a sighting of a woman's face at the top-floor window, reported by two sales assistants who were taking a break outside in the sun. Then, during the festive season of 1971, all manner of weirdness plagued the staff: the closing and opening of doors, strange thumps and bangs, as well as footsteps. It was all catalogued by manageress Marion Horne, who told Andrew Green of the oddness. For a few weeks in 1972, a strong smell of mothballs permeated the air, then suddenly ceased, and every time a supernatural occurrence took place the temperature would drop. On another occasion in the same year, another member of staff reported that having filled a drink to go with her lunch, she was dumbfounded to find it had vanished seconds later. Three other sales assistants witnessed this event.

Andrew Green believed at the time that the ghost may have been of a woman who used to live in the building when it was a block of flats. Does she still haunt the building now?

Back in the late 1990s there were two more haunted shops within Chatham's High Street. One such shop at the time was an Oxfam outlet, and upstairs many books used to line the dusty shelves. This section of the shop was said to have been haunted by an old woman, who on occasion tended to move books around just to annoy one of the male volunteers who worked there. Another shop, which is no longer in existence, used to sell books and videos, and was haunted by a phantom the staff called George – people always tend to give 'their' ghosts pet names! According to the staff, the ghost had a habit of moving objects around, although no one had ever actually seen the spook.

Maureen and the man-beast!

In 1974, one of the weirdest of supernatural encounters took place in the woodland off Sherwood Avenue in Walderslade. A woman (who I became good friends with many years later) named Maureen had ventured into the dark strip of woodland with her boyfriend (as many courting couples do), and they were attempting to construct a small fire to keep themselves warm and cosy. Maureen's boyfriend was kneeling down tending to the fire, when suddenly Maureen felt as if she was being watched. Very slowly she turned around and a few yards behind her she saw something so monstrously incomprehensible that she has never

been able to understand it to this very day. A 'creature', standing taller than a man, with an immense muscular frame and covered in hair, was watching from a thicket – its eyes glowing in the darkness. As Maureen looked at the beast it slowly lowered itself down, as if recoiling into the vegetation before disappearing from sight. A few seconds later Maureen, although terrified, rather calmly asked her boyfriend if they could leave the woods, and yet deep down she could still feel the apparition watching her. Maureen never told anyone of her encounter – not even her boyfriend – until thirty years later, when, during a conversation about strange creatures, she told me of her experience.

Interestingly, parts of what are known as Walderslade Woods have spooked people for many years. Reporting on the Your County website, a contributor named Johnny commented:

> When we were kids we played in the woods in Walderslade, and certain bits of the woods were quite odd, not so much scary, but odd. You used to go down a big gravelled hill past Tunbury school heading towards the old water towers, or towards the – what we called the motorway

In 1974 a woman had an encounter with a terrifying apparition in the woods at Walderslade. (Image created by the author)

bridge, or Meritts farm – and all the area on your right-hand side had remnants of old buildings, odd little huts, all derelict. We used to also go camping say on a Friday or Saturday night, you know with a few sausages and potatoes to cook on the fire but we always avoided the bit by the old swamp, because local saying was strange happenings went on, i.e. crunching sticks in the middle of the night, big flints being thrown through the trees. Beechin Bank and Trotts field also were always spooky, it felt as if someone was following you, watching you. This was of course before all the building had started, other bits were fine, but these spots were not quite right, probably never will be.

During the late 1980s, a group of teenagers had a frightening encounter in the woods at Walderslade. As darkness had drawn in, they decided to light a fire near a woodland path, but after a short time they grew bored and decided to move off home. Two of the group were concerned about leaving the fire roaring so they decided to head back along the pathway to put the fire out. As they reached the flickering flames both youths screamed, rushing back with haste to the rest of their mates. When the others asked the two why they'd screamed they, through gasps, stated that as they had reached the fire, a whitish 'creature' had seemed to rise up from the undergrowth and was illuminated by the orange glow of the fire. The 'beast' seemed to sit up on two legs, but was almost as tall as them. They didn't hang around to get a closer look. After telling their friends of their encounter a twig snapped in the woods, and in typical Scooby-Doo fashion, the group scrambled out of the woods, scampering in different directions to the safety of the nearby street lights.

Chased by a ghost?

At present I am a full-time monster hunter who lectures on the subject of folklore and writes books. I have had many bizarre encounters, and found myself in some peculiar situations, but never have I seen a ghost. However, when I was around twelve, I recall one summer's evening when I was playing outside my parents' house. My friend Brett was there and we'd spent the day playing football. As the night began to draw in, coming up to 10 p.m., we decided to throw a tennis ball to one another across the small green that stretched alongside the four gardens. Brett had stationed himself about 50 yards away, and I was outside of my parents' gate. We threw the ball to one another, chatting away, but due to the fading light one of my throws accidentally hit Brett full in the face. I ran over, laughing, to see if he was okay, and thankfully he was, but suddenly, from the big tree behind him, some 'thing' leapt. I'll never forget it, or the look on Brett's face, as the invisible leaper hit the floor running and came straight towards us. In terror we ran like the wind to my parents' house and stood, shaking, by the side gate of the house – but there was no sign of any ghost, ghoul, or human for that matter, but we knew that no person could leap from such a height and hit the ground running.

Another story concerning people being chased by a ghost dates back several decades and involves a group of brothers. Whilst walking home late one night from the local cinema, they passed the cemetery which backs on to Palmerstone Road. Suddenly one of them screamed in terror, and claimed that a strange, whitish shape had appeared on top of the cemetery wall and had floated towards him. Of course, his brothers never believed him and he was ridiculed, despite being a bag of nerves when he reached the safety of home. Had he seen a spectre or simply startled a nocturnal barn owl which had been resting up in the graveyard? My childhood was fuelled by ghost stories and so many of the tales I was told as a young-ster I've sadly failed to remember. However, I do recall that Chatham Cemetery (one of four in the Medway Towns), situated on Maidstone Road, was said to be haunted many years ago by a figure in white. The story was often passed around between chil-dren at varying schools, and would, no doubt, have altered over time. I do remember that a Chatham man, a bit of a strange character, used to sleep in the cemetery some nights when he had nowhere else to stay. So, maybe it was his tired, wandering form which used to be seen flitting among the gravestones, and over time

his presence was turned into a ghost story to be told around a flickering campfire.

A few decades ago my granddad, although not chased by a spectre, heard footsteps next to him one still night whilst he was walking down Palmerstone Road, as if he was being accompanied by an invisible presence. There was not a breath of wind and yet the brown leaves on the pathway were crunching as if someone was walking alongside him.

Boo! At the Bingo Hall & the phantom at the factory

The Gala Bingo Hall (Nos 324-326) in Chatham High Street used to exist as the Ritz Cinema and the Ritz Bingo Hall &

Gala Bingo Hall.

Social Club – the latter was destroyed by fire in the late 1990s and was rebuilt as the Gala Bingo Hall. Near to this was an old factory which backed on to the New Road. One old, vague ghost story pertaining to the factory mentioned how on some nights, when all was still, the machinery in the building used to start-up of its own accord. These were stories passed down through several generations, giving the area an air of mystery, even if the stories had less effect the older they got.

In his book *Ghosts of Kent*, Peter Underwood describes the bingo hall:

A building that has seen life as a cinema, a hostel and a temporary shelter for people bombed out of their homes, and a bingo hall has, according to reports, been periodically haunted for upwards of forty years. During the Second World War, when the Church Army had charge of the premises and used it as a hostel, a nearby bomb caused many casualties of varying degrees of seriousness with four people being killed, three of them children. Within months there were stories of 'strange noises' occurring in the building usually at night time (when the bombing had occurred), noises that sent chills up the spines of those who heard them for, to all intents and purposes, another bomb had fallen and again there was panic and screams of the injured and dying …

Over the years there have been reports of dying moans and muffled thuds, and a man in military uniform has, up until the 1980s, been seen upstairs. A few decades ago a cleaner caught a fleeting glimpse of the ghost, which was said to have worn a green uniform; the sound of children's voices has also been reported. According to Underwood, writing in the 1980s:

Some ten years ago a sensitive spent some time inside the property and said that she repeatedly heard the name Bill Malan clairvoyantly. She said she thought he was associated with the building when it had been a cinema and that he was the 'man in green'.

After the sightings some investigations were carried out and it was in fact proven that a man named William Malan had worked as a commissionaire at the cinema for some twenty years from 1929. Those who remember him commented how he loved the Saturday matinee and would often take care of the children. Maybe this caring soul still roams the building helping people through their day.

At No.338 High Street, and close to Gala Bingo, sits the Spotlites Theatre, housed at the Kings Theatre, a building which dates back to the nineteenth century. In November 2011, I asked Rachel Thomson-King, who runs the theatre, if there were any ghost stories attached to the building. She told me:

When a fire destroyed the Ritz Bingo Hall in 1998 we believe the ghost – who we gave the pet name George Bernard – moved into our premises for a short time. People would describe fleeting glimpses of a chap in old-fashioned clothes, or people would catch a glimpse of his back leg as he drifted by.

School ghouls

Fort Pitt Grammar School, situated on Fort Pitt Hill, has a vague ghost story which was briefly mentioned by a forum member called 'merry', on the Kent History Forum website. In August 2011 'merry' said:

This school has a very long history … The earliest bit I can recall is that there was a Roman settlement there, when I was at the school there was a human jawbone in a display case … During the Crimean war a military hospital was established there … One of my friends still swears that she saw the ghost of a lady in a crinoline dress wandering down a corridor … It was still in use as a hospital during the First World War and there are some very sad photographs of wounded soldiers sitting outside what became our English classroom.

Chatham Grammar School for Girls is also rumoured to be haunted. The school, situated on the Rainham Road, has a couple of ghosts which were mentioned in a November 2011 school newsletter put together by several students. The Main Hall is said to be haunted by an old woman. A Yoga Club exercising in the hall had their lesson disrupted by a strange old woman who stared down at them from the gallery. The leader of the class went out into the corridor to fetch the caretaker, but there was no sign of the old woman upon investigation. The Yoga Club leader then spotted a painting on the wall of an old woman, and claimed that it was the same woman who'd spooked the group. The woman in the photograph had apparently died many decades previously. An area of the school known as the 'H' corridor is said to be haunted by a young girl who loiters in the area long after all the living students have left for home. Another area of the school, known as 'H14 Landing' is prone to strange noises such as loud bangs. A few years ago, during the summer holidays, dogs belonging to a caretaker refused to enter the area and began barking for no reason.

A phantom helicopter?

A chap named Phil, who once resided at a small, quiet close in Walderslade, contacted the Your County website after a frightening experience:

On early Friday morning last [date not specified but around 2007] we here in Orbit Close were awakened at 01:45 hrs by the sound of a very low flying helicopter hovering over our houses. It was some twenty feet above the tree level. There was a bright light shining. Our house was trembling with the vibration. All the trees were blowing in the down draught. It appeared to be trying to land on the plateau. (A stretch of open scrubland next to our house.) It drifted off then returned briefly (not as close) and disappeared.

The next day I went to the press and Rochester airport. The traffic controller denied it was from that airport. At the reported level it was below the radar range so nothing was picked up. The police denied everything; they claimed it was the air ambulance. The air ambulance fly between 07:00 and 19:00 hrs only (so they say). A special branch detective rang and said there was no trace of any aircraft around at that time. He did say that a workmate of his, who lives in Penenden Heath heard a helicopter flying around at that time. He stated that it was probably a rogue aircraft and an investigation is under way by the authorities. He said it was not the military and the relevant bodies have been advised. The 'x files' of it all is that it was flying so low to keep out of radar range. How then if it was so low did it avoid the pylons and masts over the top of the hill on route to or from Penenden Heath? They said that 70ft is well below the radar range. This is below the height of the pylons and masts also.

It was downright scary and very dangerous. I thought that there was to be a crash.

A Chatham ghostly ballad

The fourth volume (of twelve) of the *Bygone Kent* series features an article called 'Ballads of Kent', by Carson Ritchie. The feature begins: 'In the days before newspapers, Kent folk relied on the printed ballad for some of the current news of the day, and for a great deal of the interest in what were often drab lives.'

Whilst simple ballads were very popular, Ritchie comments that: 'The kind of ballads that sold well were sensational ones, songs about murders, hangings and suicides.' One such ballad, called 'The Chatham Tragedy', features a local girl called Mary Fletcher. According to the song, Mary pledged her undying love to a seaman by breaking a gold coin with him, so that when he went off to sea, they

Woodcut depicting the ghostly ballad of Chatham.

would never feel apart because they would each hold a half of the coin. However, when the seaman failed to return home after a very long time, the forlorn Mary Fletcher found love elsewhere, and fell into the arms of a farmer's son. Well, you can imagine the dismay of the seaman when he finally returned home only to discover that his soulmate had left him. So depressed was he that he hanged himself on the tree which faced her house. The ballad, according to Ritchie's article states, '... his ghost appeared to her as she was in bed, whereupon she arose and followed him, and never has been heard of since.'

Terror at the Town Hall

The Town Hall of Chatham, situated at The Brook – and which now harbours the Brook Theatre, a 400-seat auditorium – was built in 1900. This rather Gothic-looking building is, unsurprisingly, haunted. The Historic Medway website mentions a few ghost stories passed on from an Ann Barrett, who was Director of the Medway Arts Centre from 1989 to 1996. She told the website, '[I] can tell you of very strange events taking place in the building. I was often called out by the police in the middle of the night for supposed break-ins – but all I encountered were ghosts and the like ...'

According to Ann, the basement was, and still is, littered with bricked-up tunnels which allegedly ran from the Naval Hospital, situated near the Great Lines – the imposing hillside which overlooks Chatham. She commented:

There were lots of stories – but all I can say is that I saw the nurse in old-fashioned uniform. The Theatre, formerly

Chatham Town Hall.

the Ballroom, is extremely haunted; the building is known to be one of the most haunted places in Kent. We kept this very quiet so as to not alarm the users and visitors which included many children.

Despite Ann's claims that there are 'lots of stories', when I enquired at the booking office about resident ghosts, I was given a rather perplexed look by the booking attendant. She responded, under her breath, that 'ghostly soldiers' had been seen in the basement, but sadly she could not elaborate any further.

The ghoul on the hill – the Great Lines spook

'The Fool On The Hill', a track written by The Beatles for their Magical Mystery Tour

The Great Lines which loom over Chatham.

album reminds me of a ghost encounter I was told about as a child by my relative Joe Chester. The incident occurred whilst he was walking over the Great Lines (the Great Lines are more than 70 hectares of green space which loom over Chatham). Some areas of this green space are said to harbour Roman remains. A few years ago at Upbury Farm, near the Chatham Lines, twelve skeletons were excavated. James Presnail, writing in *The Story Of Chatham*, stated that: 'The town and the neighbouring Dockyard are defended by formidable and extensive ranges of military works, denominated the Lines.'

Also, a large Royal Naval war memorial sits atop the Lines. It was erected in 1924 in dedication to those sailors from Chatham-based ships who lost their lives in both World Wars. More than 8,000 names can be read on the plaques.

As a teenager, Joe used to work in a shop called Babyland, situated on Duncan Road in Gillingham. At the time, Joe had no transport and thus he had to deliver prams across Medway by hand so, to say that he was knackered by the time he'd finished a day's toil was an understatement. Then, after work he would have to suffer the walk home, which would take him once more across the Great Lines, often in the dark. One evening, as Joe whistled away his journey home, he noticed a man wearing a trilby hat and a long raincoat, standing perfectly still, and staring across Chatham town from the Lines. Joe recounts: 'He just stood there, quite still, at first merely some black silhouette … I was feeling a little uneasy as I neared him, and almost decided to take another path home.'

As Joe got closer to the man, he thought to himself, 'Surely he's heard me approaching …', but the man continued to silently gaze ahead across the valley. As Joe got to

within a few metres, suddenly, the man completely vanished into thin air.

'I hurriedly made my way down the grassy bank to the hill we had referred to as Mark Packer's Hill, and over the High Street, through the library alley, across the New Road into the safety of my house,' said Joe.

Recalling that strange encounter, Joe concluded recently, ' … it had been no hallucination. What I had seen had been another ghost. No one will ever convince me otherwise.'

The lady of the graves

One of Chatham's vaguest ghost stories pertains to the old graves which sit in the Town Hall gardens. Whiffens Avenue, which runs alongside the Town Hall, has a car park which backs on to the burial ground. Due to overcrowding in the churchyard of St Mary's Church, Dock Road, a new cemetery was opened at Whiffens Avenue in 1828. Burials took place here up until 1870. When the area was opened as the Town Hall gardens, the graves were moved against the flanking walls. On an autumnal afternoon, the ivy-strewn and ashen tombstones, often dappled by the sun, make for

A ghostly lady is said to wander amongst the graves behind the Town Hall.

quite a Gothic backdrop – contradicted, almost, by the children's play area just a few metres away! The ghost story, albeit a brief one, concerns a young woman in a long, whitish gown who was once said to be known as the 'lady of the tombstones'. Her forlorn figure was occasionally said to wander amongst the jutting stones, but no one knows who she is.

The Town Hall gardens are one of Chatham's best-kept secrets. This tranquil place is often frequented by dog walkers and those who wish to relax on the benches dotted about the place. Goodness knows how many souls rest beneath their feet. The Medway Memories website features a story:

Mr Collins, who lived in Nelson Road — which was demolished to make way for the Pentagon — says: 'In 1941, the Army dug a tank trap in the area above Chatham Town Hall gardens. They uncovered a lot of lead coffins containing the bodies of soldiers from Victorian times — probably victims of some sort of epidemic. A lot of the coffins were broken open and put in a heap. I 'rescued' a skull, took it home, varnished it and then took it to my school, Highfields, and presented it to the science teacher.'

What a great schoolboy souvenir!

The school put it in a glass cabinet, but its whereabouts are now unknown – it vanished probably when a new school was built on the site.

The original entrance on Whiffens Lane boasts an engraved slab which reads:

To

The Memory Of

Patrick Feeney

Sergeant Of The 50th Regiment

Who Died 9th July 1834

Aged 31 Years

He Was Shot On That Day By

Benjamin Gardiner

A Private Of The Same Company In

The Evening In Chatham Barracks

For Which The Murderer Was Hanged

On Chatham Lines In The Presence Of

The Troops Of The Chatham Garrison

This Stone Was Erected By The Officers

Of The 50th Regiment To Mark The Worth

Patrick Feeney's

Character Was Held In By Them

The legend of St Mary's

St Mary's Church sits on Dock Road, within a few yards of Fort Amherst. Edwin Harris, writing about the church, said, 'At what period a church was erected in this district cannot be discovered', but it was destroyed by fire during the fourteenth century and rebuilt. In fact, the church was rebuilt on several occasions after – during one of these constructions, or so it is rumoured, the headless figure of a virgin holding a child was discovered. However, the truth of the matter is that an ancient slab was found embedded in the Norman wall of the chapel, and this depicted the Greek goddess, Euphrosyne, a mythical nymph. The figure on the marble

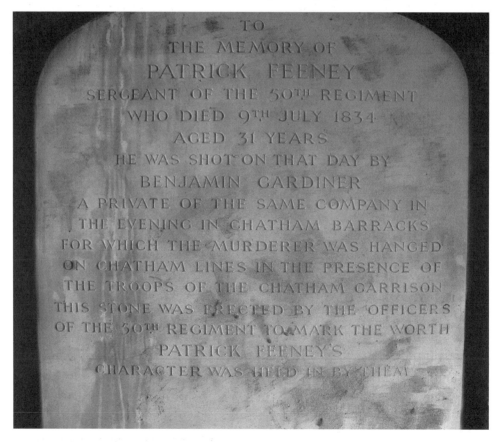

Plaque dedicated to the memory of Patrick Feeney.

slab appeared bereft of head, and was believed to be more than 2,000 years old. At the time of the discovery the slab was said to have been 'the oldest thing in the Medway Towns.'

In 1772 a human hand, clutching the brass hilt of a sword, was discovered in the churchyard. On a mild, autumnal day the church peeks over the rustic treetops, and coupled with the carpet of leaves below, the setting is perfect for a ghost story.

The legend that pertains to St Mary's Church is a very old one and concerns 'Our Lady of Chatham', who, according to the story, 'In Roman Catholic times was highly celebrated for her miracles'. Some legends state that the woman – the Virgin Mary – was in fact an apparition. Kentish historian Lambarde, in his *A Perambulation of Kent*, published in 1570, records the folktale as follows:

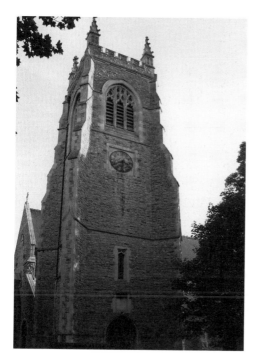

St Mary's Church.

Although I have not hitherto at any time read any memorable thing recorded in historee touching Chetham itselfe, yet, for so much as I have often heard (and that constantly) reported, a Popish illusion done at this place, and for that also it is as profitable to the keeping under of fained and superstitious religion, to renew to mind the Priestly practices of olde time (which are now declining to oblivion) as it is pleasant to reteine in memorie the Monuments and Antiquities of whatsoever other kinde, I thinke it not amisse to commit faithfully in writing, what I have received credibly by hearing, concerning the Idols, sometime knowen by the names, of our Lady and the Roode, of Chatham, and Gillingham.

It happened (say they) that the dead Corps of a man (lost through shipwracke belike) was cast on land in the Parish of Chetham and being there taken up, was by some charitable persons committed to honest burial within their Churchyards; which thing was no sooner done, but our Lady of Chetham, finding her selfe offended therwith, arose by night, and went in person to the house of the parishe Clearke, (which then was in the Streets a good distrance from the Church) and making a noise at is windowe awaked him. This man at the first (as commonly it fareth with men disturbed in their rest) demaunded somewhat roughly who was there: But when he understoode by hir owne aunswere, that it was the Lady of Chetham, hee changed his note, and most mildely asked the cause of her good Ladisgips coming: She told him, that there was lately buried (neare to the place where she was honoured) a sinfull person, which so offended her eie with his ghastly grinning, that unlesse he were removed, she could not but (to the great griefe of good people) withdraw her selfe from that place, and cease her wonted miraculous working amongst them. And therefore she willed him to go with her, to the end that (by his helpe) she might take him up and cast him againe into the River.

The Clerke obeid, arose and waited on her toward the Church, but the good Ladie (not wonted to walke) waxed wearie of the labour, and therefore was inforced for very want of breath to sit downe in a bush by the way, and there to rest her; And this place (forsooth) as also the whole tracke of their journey (remaining ever after a greene path) the Towne dwellers were wont to shew. Now after a while, they go forward againe, and coming to the Churchyard, digged up the body, and conveied it to the water side, where it was first found. This done, our Lady shranke againe into her shrine, and the Clearke peaked home to patch up his broken sleepe, but the corps now eftsoones floted up and downe the River, as it did before. Which thing being at length espied by them of Gillingham, it was once more taken up and buried in their Churchyard. But see what followed upon it, not onely the Roode of Gillingham (say they) that a while before was busie in bestowing Miracles, was now deprived of all that his former virtue: but also the very earth and place where the carcasse was laide, did continually for ever after, settle and sinke doweward. This tale received by tradition from the Elders, was (long since) both commonly reported and faithfully credited of the vulgar sort: which although happily you shall not at this day learne at every mans mouth (the Image being now many yeeres sithence defaced) yet many of the aged number did lately remember it well, and in the time of darknesse, Hæc erat in toto notissima fibula mundo. But here (if I might be so bold as to adde to this Fable (or Fabula significant) I would tell you, that I thought the Morall and Minde of the tale to bee none other, but that this Clerkly, this Talewright (I say) and Fableforger, being either the Ferner, or Owner of the offrings given to our Lady of Chetham, and envying the common haunt and Pilgrimage to the Roode of Gillingham (lately erected Ad nocumentum of this gaine) devised this apparition, for the advauncement of the one, and defacing of the other.

For (no doubt) if that age had beene as prudent in examining spirits, as it was prone to believe illusions, it should have found, that our Ladies path was some such greene trace of grasse, as we daily behold in the fields (proceeding in deede of a naturall cause, though by olde wives and superstitious people reckoned to be the daucing places of night spirits, which they call Fayries). And that this sinking grave, was nothing else, but a false filled pitte of Maister Clearks owne digging.

Interestingly, Howell's *The Kentish Note Book* records, several centuries later, the legend as that of the 'Lady of Gillingham'.

The man in the hospital

All Saints' Hospital, formerly Medway Union Workhouse, was built in 1849, and was demolished during the late 1990s. It was situated on Magpie Hall Road but the site now harbours houses. In 1961 my great-grandfather, William George Arnold, lay on his deathbed at the hospital. He was suffering from cancer. Late on a Thursday night my great-grandfather saw, standing at the bottom of his bed, an elderly man with a white beard.

'Are you John Arnold?' my great-grandfather asked, but the figure disappeared.

The following night my great-grandfather passed away, but not before telling my granddad of what he'd seen. My granddad asked his mother if she knew of a John Arnold, and she replied that he was her father in-law.

Spirit in the sky

In my book, *Shadows in the Sky: The Haunted Airways of Britain*, I looked at varying aerial phenomena such as ghost planes, UFOs and the appearance of what are deemed 'angels'. During the end of the First World War, my great-grandmother, Lily Lydia, had a sighting of an apparition in the sky over her home at The Mount in Chatham. On 22 and 23 August, as British troops battled the enemy in Belgium, an angelic type of entity was said to have appeared in the skies over Chatham, and it became known as the 'Angel of Mons'. Many perceived this figure as a sign of good luck, and believed that it signalled the end of the war. My great-grandmother told my grandfather that she'd observed this spirit and that a few days later the war had ended. However, sceptics have argued that such a form – albeit one that was witnessed by many soldiers – was simply a cloud. There was even a rumour that the figure was a projection cast on to the clouds by the Germans to confuse the British troops – but, according to legend, this plan backfired and the apparition merely spurred the soldiers on. The 'angel' my great-grandmother saw was not simply a misinterpretation of anatural phenomenon, because the figure

During the end of the First World War my great-grandmother, Lily Lydia, observed an angel in the sky over her home at The Mount. (Image created by the author)

was also seen over Peckham, in London, by several witnesses, and this incident was reported on by the *South London Times*.

According to my granddad, Lily Lydia was a very down-to-earth woman and not prone to flights of fancy. I believe she was one of the fortunate ones who observed a spirit symbolising forthcoming peace.

Spirit in the salon

During the late 1990s and early 2000s, a Mr Chris Cooke was manager of an undisclosed hair salon, situated just off Chatham's High Street. In September 2011 he told me of two unusual incidents which had spooked him at the salon.

> One afternoon we had something slightly odd happen in the kitchen area when a kettle, of its own accord, just fell over. The kettle had never fallen over before and there was no vibration etc. to cause this, but the strangest thing happened during one Christmas. When we shut up for the festive holidays a box of amaretto biscuits were left on a shelf. They were there for four days. I went back after the holiday and was working alone when I suddenly heard a crash on the floor. When I entered the room the biscuits were on the floor, but there's no way they could have slid off. It was odd.

Whilst sceptics may find it easy to dismiss such stories, these things happen regularly to people all over the world – items moving of their own accord, objects disappearing then reappearing and such. Whether this is the work of mischievous ghosts we'll never really know, but when there is no rational explanation for such events, they must remain a mystery.

Things that come in the night

My final supernatural story could well be the weirdest and most chilling entry in this volume of ghostly tales. It concerns a Chatham man, who, whilst in his early twenties, was settling down to sleep one night at his home in Walderslade, when he felt something on the middle finger of his left hand. Thinking an insect had crawled into his bed, the man glanced at his hand expecting to see a pea bug or some type of arachnid. But what he saw made him gasp in horror. There, on his finger, was a black 'object', the size of a tennis ball, that seemed to be pulling at his finger. Alarmed by the thing in the bed, the man slammed his hand down hard on the mattress but could not shake the intruder. After several attempts at ridding his finger of the monstrosity, the critter seemed to vanish, leaving the startled witness with not only a sore finger but a pool of blood in the bed.

Now, those among you who are not prone to flights of fancy may be quick to blame this incident on a bad dream or an intrusive insect, but this wasn't the only time such a thing took place. A couple of years later the same witness was snuggling down into his bed at around midnight when he felt something move at the bottom of the bed. One thing worth remembering is that the witness had not fallen asleep, but had simply got into bed, so this could not have been a nightmare. The witness, recalling the incident of the black bob a few years before, stood up in bed and noticed a weird, translucent object perched on his right shoulder. The object was the size and rough shape of a rugby ball, but the critter had stubby appendages on both of its flanks. In absolute panic, the witness swiped at the apparition with his right hand and the amorphous blob seemed to fade, leaving him with a tingling left arm.

Unnerved by the incident, the man told his parents what he'd seen. Then a few days later, the witness' father was sitting on the living-room floor reading a newspaper when a whitish 'blob' seemed to float from the direction of the bedroom where the incident had taken place, before vanishing into thin air.

A cousin of the witness reported a similar incident around the same time. The witness, who I'll call 'J', had just finished reading in bed and had turned the light out when suddenly a voice whispered, 'Is it okay?' into his ear. Suddenly, 'J' felt something drop on to the foot of the bed. When he looked down he saw a tennis ball-sized black blob. In terror, the man kicked at the object, which seemed to hover up to the window and then simply fade. 'J' tried to rationally explain the incident but it could not have been a bird or insect as the window was closed, and the object did not move like either and had vanished into thin air.

Surprisingly, this type of bedroom encounter − known as night terrors − is relatively common and occurs the world over. A scientific term applied to this is 'sleep paralysis', and usually involves a sole witness who, whilst asleep on their back, wakes in the night but cannot move. They then sense a presence in the room which only they can see − and this presence is said to apply a crushing weight to the chest of the victim. The hold of the entity is only broken when the frozen witness manages to move

Some of the eeriest ghost stories are best confined to old buildings.

a limb or blink an eye. During the 1990s, a young family on the Weedswood Estate was plagued by eerie activity, which seemed to centre itself on the female of the couple. On several occasions she awoke at night to hear heavy breathing next to the bed. On another occasion the flapping of wings was heard.

In folklore, bedroom encounters of this ilk are called the 'old hag syndrome'. Witnesses often describe being molested or crushed by an old hag-like crone who enters their room at night. In other cases witnesses, whilst unable to move, report seeing shadowy figures, and in a majority of these cases, witnesses describe being drained of energy. These encounters echo legends of the incubus and succubus, which are male and female demons – the male demon is said to molest females, and the succubus molests men.

Scientific study into the phenomenon of such bedroom invaders has, as yet, been unable to explain why witnesses are seemingly attacked in their sleep. Stress, bad diet, overtiredness, are just some of the factors scientists have highlighted, but none of these states should evoke such nightmarish apparitions.

This complex phenomenon may well have connections to the human psyche, or, rather worryingly, suggest that when the human body relaxes toward or during slumber, it is prone to astral manifestations and prey to other ethereal scavengers. My advice – sleep with one eye open.

And this is where the jaunt through haunted Chatham ends. Blow out the candle and sleep well.

They asked for my story. I have told it. Enough.

Susan Hill – *The Woman in Black*

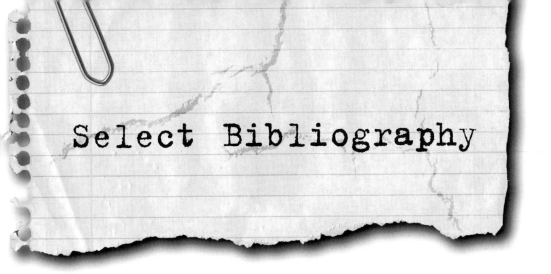

Select Bibliography

Books & Magazines

Arnold, N., *Mystery Animals of the British Isles: Kent* (CFZ Press, 2009)

Chester, J., *Haunted Kent* (Privately published, 1997)

Green, A., *Haunted Kent Today* (S.B. Publications, 1999)

Green, A., *Our Haunted Kingdom* (Fontana, 1974)

Harris, E., *The History of St Mary's Church, Chatham* (?)

Hervey, M., *They Walk By Night* (Ace Books, 1968)

Hippisley Cox, A.D., *Haunted Britain* (Pan, 1973)

Howell, G.O., *The Kentish Note Book Vol. I* (Henry Gray, 1894)

Johnson, W.H., *Kent Stories of the Supernatural* (Countryside Books, 2000)

Matthews, R., *Ghost Hunter Walks in Kent* (S.B. Publications, 2005)

Matthews, R., *Haunted Places of Kent* (Countryside Books, 2004)

Paine, B. & Sturgess, T., *Unexplained Kent* (Breedon, 1997)

Presnail, J., *The Story of Chatham* (Corporation of Chatham, 1952)

Ritchie, C., *Bygone Kent,* Vol. 12, No. 4, pp. 205–208 (Meresborough Books, 1991)

Underwood, P., *A Gazetteer of British Ghosts* (Pan, 1971)

Underwood, P., *Ghosts of Kent* (Meresborough, 1985)

Websites

www.bluebellhillghostwalk.blogspot.com

www.fortamherst.com

www.ghostconnections.com

www.ghostsearchuk.com

www.hauntedrochester.blogspot.com

www.historicmedway.co.uk

www.kenthistoryforum.co.uk

www.medwaymemories.co.uk

www.paranormalmagazine.co.uk

www.roadghosts.com

www.thedockyard.co.uk

www.yourcounty.co.uk

If you enjoyed this book, you may also be interested in…

Shadows in the Sky: The Haunted Airways of Britain
NEIL ARNOLD

Although the saying, 'Pigs might fly' may bring a smile to one's lips, even stranger things ha
been reported as appearing in Britain's skies over the centuries. Eyewitnesses have testifi
that various terrifying and bizarre forms have appeared in the skies, from ghostly plan
phantom airships and UFOs, to reports of sky serpents, celestial dragons – even reports
a griffin seen over London! *Shadows in the Sky* compiles hundreds of accounts from t
spine-chilling to the downright bizarre, that'll keep your eyes fixed looking upwards!

978 0 7524 6563 0

Haunted Ashford
NEIL ARNOLD

From screaming woods and hellhounds to phantom planes, poltergeists and apparitions, t
collection of hauntings – which includes stories from Pluckley, reputedly Britain's mo
ghost-infested village – unearths the ghostly secrets of Ashford, the heart of the 'Gard
of England'. Featuring an array of haunted priories, public houses, castles and churchya
including many spiritual encounters that have never appeared in print before, *Haun
Ashford* will delight everyone with an interest in the darker side of the area's history.

978 0 7524 6127 4

Haunted Maidstone
NEIL ARNOLD

For the first time, the historic town of Maidstone gives up its darkest and eeriest secr
Including previously unpublished accounts of ghostly activity and re-examining clas
cases, this is a treasure trove of original material and atmospheric photography. From ta
of haunted buildings to ghosts witnessed on winding roads. With a foreword by Sean Tud
the Blue Bell Hill ghost expert, it unravels stories which will send a shiver down the spi
of any resident, historian or ghost-hunter.

978 0 7524 5922 6

Paranormal Kent
NEIL ARNOLD

Kent has long been known as the 'Garden of England'; however, this idyllic corner
Britain also has its darker side. This richly illustrated book covers a fascinating range
strange events. From sightings of big cats, UFOs, monsters and fairies to terrifying tales
dragon encounters and phantom hitchhikers, this incredible volume will invite the rea
to view the area in a whole new light. *Paranormal Kent* will delight all those interested
the mysteries of the paranormal.

978 0 7524 5590 7

Visit our website and discover thousands of other History Press books.
www.thehistorypress.co.uk